Amidst the ~~Gladiolas~~

by Vito Gentile

A SAMUEL FRENCH ACTING EDITION

SAMUEL FRENCH

FOUNDED 1830

NEW YORK HOLLYWOOD LONDON TORONTO

SAMUELFRENCH.COM

ISBN 978-0-573-60571-0   Printed in U.S.A.   #3073

MUSIC USE NOTE

IMPORTANT BILLING AND CREDIT
REQUIREMENTS

AMIDST THE GLADIOLAS, a Prism Theatre, Inc., production, Steven Stewart-James, producer, in association with Harold Bligh, opened at the Lion Theatre, on New York City's Theatre Row, October 26, 1981. The cast, in order of appearance, was as follows:

MRS. FRANCINE DEFANIE	Dorothy Holland
SAMMY LUCCHESE	Joe Palmieri
BERNARD	James Selby
MRS. CONNIE BARBALOTTIO	Sally-Jame Heit*
MRS. MARYANNE LONGO	Rosemary Prinz
MISS PHYLLIS BATTISTA	Estelle Kelmer
MRS. ROSE GUTTA	Esther Brandice
MRS. JENNY BARBALOTTIO	Dina Paisner

Director – Ron Comenzo
Set Designer – Robert R. Yodice
Floral Designer - Joe Lucchese
Costume Co-ordinators – Eileen Madison, Judith Couzens**
Lighting Designer – Tom Gould
Production Stage Manager – D.C. Rosenberg
Stage Manager – Kathleen Masters
Technical Director – Bernadette Wise
Press Representative – Clarence Allsopp
Production Manager – Arturo E. Porazzi
Graphic Designer – Rick Ellis

*Eleni Kiamos replaced Ms. Heit in the role of Connie on December 25, 1981.

**Sam Fleming, Costume Designer, replaced the Costume Co-ordinators on November 22 1981.

PLAYWRIGHT'S NOTES

AMIDST THE GLADIOLAS is a drama laced with innate laughs, as well as quiet moments of reflection. Its characters are highly charged, which makes them prone to jump on each other's lines in a scrap, to relish a good laugh, or to descend into pathos with equal gusto. And between this trio of emotional highs and lows there are long silences to reenergize.

And since the play runs in real time, pacing is everything and the clock's chimes have been set in place to protect these parameters. Where dialogue is designated "whispered," it is meant to be not fully audible to the audience. While they strain their ears, let them strain their eyes too.

The lighting should be low. Sound is also important; the offstage clock tolling, the muffled voices out in the lobby, the eerie motor of a service elevator, and police car doors slamming in the street with the added visual of red rotating beacons flashing through a window all lend an element of truth. As to the casket; it is a powerful presence, especially when draped in a flag. Beware of its impact and sense of reverence.

Italian words are in italics and brackets () have been used for translations and other clarification only. For the adventurous, a copy with the original Neapolitan dialect is also available.

Lastly, *AMIDST THE GLADIOLAS* is not about Brooklyn accents. Don't use one even if you were born there. All the "Brooklyn" you'll need has been built into the rhythm of the piece, and there are enough words like "ain't," "gotta," "ya," and "gladiolas" to give your interpretation authenticity.

AMIDST THE GLADIOLAS is the first part of the trilogy *Francine in Black and White*. Its companion pieces are *Confetti and Italian Ice*, and *Cold Manhattan Special*.

– Vito Gentile

CHARACTERS

(in order of appearance)

FRANCINE – A thirty-three year-old fragile and pregnant Polish-Italian-American.

SAMMY – A slick, balding, Italian-American undertaker in his late forties.

BERNARD – A flamboyant twenty-eight year-old Italian-American undertaker.

CONNIE – a forty year-old tough Italian-American blond.

MARYANNE – A sharp-witted Italian-American hairdresser in her late forties.

PHYLLIS – An artless Italian-American hairdresser in her late forties.

ROSA – A large intimidating Italian-American woman in her sixties.

JENNY – A venomous Neapolitan beauty in her seventies.

ACT ONE

*(**THE SCENE**: The Gold Room at Lucchese's Funeral Home, Carroll Gardens, Brooklyn, New York – August 1981.)*

(This formerly grand room sits at street level in a nineteenth-century brownstone. At one end full-length draperies hang on a wall designed to softly frame a bier, as well as conceal a set of windows. A table for remembrance cards stands before them, and a usually concealed service elevator at the far end is seen where a portion of the draperies have been pulled open. Above, a series of spotlights accentuate the area. A smoking alcove at the end of a private hall stands on a raised platform. It has large windows with tie-back draperies facing the street, and contains two occasional chairs and a pedestal ashtray. A light dimmer is discreetly hidden near its entrance. Dominating the main room are a pair of large double doors that lead to the lobby. A guest register book stand is to their right, and to their left, ten closed wooden folding chairs lean against the wall alongside a large, imposing – yet somewhat tattered – easy-chair. The room's ample center remains empty.)

*(**IT IS SUGGESTED THAT**: Gerald Finzi's Clarinet Concerto – part one: Allegro Vigoroso, or a similar thought-provoking secular piece be played to set the mood as the house lights dim.)*

*(**AT RISE**: Strong shafts of sunlight shoot thought the alcove windows and deny the observer a view of the street and beyond.)*

(As the somber music fades and the sunlight dims, two red rotating police car beacons whizz by the windows quickly followed by a third, which stops and hovers for

7

a moment until a car door slams and it too zooms off.
MRS. FRANCINE DEFANIE, *a Polish-Italian-American
thirty-three year-old enters through the main lobby doors.
Six months pregnant, the emotionally fragile* **FRANCINE**
*wears a bright polka-dot maternity dress, carries a purse,
and a large dark blue men's sweater with a NYPD patch
which she clutches to her bosom. Surveying the vast near-
empty room, she crosses to the smoking alcove and folds
into a chair with her head down. The sound of the arriv-
ing service elevator panics her, and she jumps from the
chair and backs away, creating a silhouette in front of
the sunlit windows.)*

*(***SAMMY LUCCHESE***, an Italian-American in his late
forties, enters from the service elevator. He is balding
and wears an ill-fitting new suit.* **BERNARD***, a well-
dressed twenty-eight year-old Italian-American enters
behind him, whistling a fragmented version of "You and
the Night and the Music." Together they wheel a bronze
casket out of the elevator. A freshly pressed American flag
is folded across the casket's center. Both are stunned to
find* **FRANCINE** *waiting in the smoking alcove.)*

SAMMY. Francine!

(to **BERNARD***)*

Get the flowers!

*(***BERNARD** *hurries off in the elevator and the sound of
it descending fills the room.* **FRANCINE** *gingerly crosses
towards the casket but* **SAMMY** *blocks her path.)*

Francine, how are you? You should have called. We
would have sent someone to get you.

FRANCINE. Every time I looked out there were more and
more. If I didn't come now –

SAMMY. I understand. I understand. You'll have to excuse
us, with so many things we have to do – you can see
we're not ready.

*(***SAMMY***, with his best professional manner, leads* **FRAN-
CINE** *back to the smoking alcove.)*

SAMMY. *(cont.)* Maybe you'd like to use the ladies room? Freshen up? Give us about two minutes.

(As he pivots her towards the private hall...)

He was a good person and a good friend.

(nudging her forward)

Use the one downstairs – it's more private.

*(**FRANCINE** exits. **SAMMY** rushes back to the main room and glides the casket to its proper place against the wall. He then crosses to the big easy-chair and places it carefully at an angle to the casket. He then takes two folding chairs and places them directly in front of the casket near the big chair. Next, he grabs three more folding chairs and places them evenly behind the first two. He then takes a breath before running back to retrieve three more and starts a second set, aligning them with the first. Exhausted, he runs back and retrieves the last two chairs and places them behind the three he has just placed. **BERNARD** enters from the elevator carrying a large floral arrangement of plastic gladioli.)*

BERNARD. I thought this was going to be a classy funeral.

SAMMY. The Pope saying the Mass – that ain't enough for you?

BERNARD. I'm talking about this!

SAMMY. He's not going to see them. He's only saying the Mass.

BERNARD. Only two days in New York and you think he has nothing better to do?

SAMMY. Hey, this guy saved his life! The Pope's got obligations just like anyone else.

BERNARD. What obligations? People shoot him, and he wears a paper hat *(miter)*. Look at this – the pistils are all covered with crud.

SAMMY. They'll do! When their flowers come we'll get them out of here. Put them in the corner.

BERNARD. I should put them in the street.

(As he places the gladioli under a spotlight near the head of the casket…)

Maybe we should use the Pink Room? The ceiling isn't peeling in there.

SAMMY. Francine, she had her mother, her father, Carmine – God knows who else in here. People are funny about things like that.

*(**BERNARD** crosses to the casket and unfolds the American flag, but the draping of it causes difficulty.)*

BERNARD. I don't know why they insist on using these things, they never hang right.

*(As **SAMMY** slaps the top of the casket…)*

SAMMY. That baby is solid bronze! You think I want it covered?

BERNARD. Our best casket covered with a three-ninety-nine flag. No one likes to pay for something they can't see.

*(**SAMMY** eyes the casket's position.)*

SAMMY. Give me a hand.

*(Together they move the casket a notch. As **BERNARD** points to a stain on the draperies…)*

BERNARD. What about this stain?

SAMMY. Shit!

*(They return the casket to its original position. **SAMMY** crosses to a light dimmer and lowers the lights.)*

That's better.

*(As **BERNARD** retrieves the remembrance card table…)*

BERNARD. You expect people to see in here or sleep?

*(**SAMMY** raises the lights slightly. As **BERNARD** sets the table for remembrance cards at the foot of the casket…)*

They're going to need more than that for the cameras. They need light – lots of it.

SAMMY. No cameras! No pictures in the chapel! You hear me?! No pictures in the chapel!

BERNARD. Of course, Mr. Lucchese!

SAMMY. You know reporters; they'll snap every crack in here!

BERNARD. We can't have that, can we?

SAMMY. Don't be smart!

*(**BERNARD** crosses to the elevator and fetches a wooden kneeler.)*

Bernard, use the better one.

BERNARD. For His Holiness! My mistake – I should have gone on vacation!

*(**BERNARD**, with kneeler, exits in the elevator.)*

SAMMY. *(calling after him)* What? You want to go work in Manhattan – go! Big mouth bastard!

*(**SAMMY** crosses to the gladioli, whips out his hand-kerchief and tries to clear the dust from the pedals. **FRANCINE** enters from the private hall and pauses in the smoking alcove.)*

Francine, come in. It's alright.

*(**FRANCINE** turns towards the windows.)*

You got to be strong at a time like this – for your baby – God bless ya!

(ref: the crowd outside)

Don't worry about them. They're just curious – nothing to get upset over.

FRANCINE. I know. Nothing!

*(**SAMMY** crosses to her.)*

SAMMY. Once they see someone, so they can say they saw them, they'll go.

(She cries and he steps back patiently waiting for her sobs to subside.)

(taking her hand)

SAMMY. *(cont.)* I understand. I understand. Francine, these are the ways of the Lord. It was Joe's blessed destiny to lay down his own life to save that of the Holy Father.

(He leads a hesitant **FRANCINE** *down to the big easy-chair in front of the casket.)*

Come on, sit down.

(She sits, and he patiently waits for her to familiarize herself to her new surroundings. Once she's comfortable he shrewdly lifts the edge of the flag and reveals the casket underneath.)

It's the best we have. Just like you requested! God bless him. God love him.

(Knowing she is watching him, the skilled **SAMMY** *turns to the casket, lowers his head in silent prayer, and then closes the moment by adding the perfect measure of profound grief – a handkerchief dab to an eye.)*

(turning to her)

If there is anything you want –

*(***BERNARD** *enters from the private hall carrying a fancy kneeler. On his way to the casket he deliberately crosses in front of* **SAMMY** *and interrupts his shtick. As an annoyed* **SAMMY** *fumes, the fastidious* **BERNARD** *places the "grand" kneeler in front of the casket in the grandest of manner and then draws the draperies in front of the elevator. He leisurely exits down the private hall. Once* **SAMMY** *knows* **BERNARD** *has safely gone, he continues his shtick. As* **SAMMY** *speaks, in the smoking alcove windows behind him many rotating police car beacons appear and turn the windows a bright red. The sound of many car doors slamming follows. Then the red beacons whizz off.)*

If there is anything you want, just ask. You don't like something, tell me. That's what I'm here for.

(An anxious **FRANCINE** *clutches her sweater.)*

The air conditioning too high?

FRANCINE. It's fine.

SAMMY. If you get too cold, I'll lower it. I don't want you catching a cold. I might sound like a mother hen, but this is no time for you to be fooling around with the flu.

*(**FRANCINE** musters up a smile.)*

You're feeling better already.

(Offstage a clock strikes one o'clock, followed by chimes.)

*(**SAMMY** checks his wristwatch.)*

(irate) You're an hour early?

FRANCINE. I wanted to be first.

SAMMY. *(covering his annoyance)* I understand. I understand.

(As he sits down next to her...)

By the way, I didn't put the usual notice in the News. I didn't want you wasting your money for nothing – the wording *(would be difficult)...*

FRANCINE. *(whispering)* Oh!

SAMMY. You know Francine, there's a rumor the Pope might stop back in New York for Joe's mass. I mean it's on his way home. Let's face it; the least he could do is stop by. Well, let me leave you.

(as he stands)

Remember, I'm just outside.

FRANCINE. Sammy –

SAMMY. Yes?

FRANCINE. How can I repay you for all you've done?

SAMMY. Just put a smile on that pretty face – the way he liked to see ya.

(making the sign of the cross)

God bless him. What could you do?

*(**SAMMY** crosses to the draperies in front of the elevator, closes them, and moves the remembrance card table in front of the closed draperies. Spying the cracked ceiling he*

*crosses to the dimmer in the smoking alcove and lowers
the lights. After a quick survey of the room, he exits to the
main lobby and gently closes the doors behind him.)*

(After a long pause, **FRANCINE** *stands. Using her
sweater as a security blanket, she musters the strength
and gingerly makes her journey to the casket, but freezes
when the main lobby doors swing open forcefully.* **MRS.
CONNIE BARBALOTTIO**, *a forty year-old Italian-American dressed in full mourning – including a mourning
veil over her face – enters in a huff from the main
lobby, amid the sound of many muffled voices coming
from same.* **FRANCINE** *turns, seeing the figure in black,
quickly returns to the big chair and places her sweater
and purse in her lap. As* **CONNIE** *slams the door...)*

CONNIE. Animals!

*(****CONNIE*** *rips the mourning veil off her head revealing a
mop of freshly dyed platinum blond hair and a face-full
of makeup. As she adjusts her clothes, she spies the figure
in the big chair.)*

Francine!

(crossing to **FRANCINE***)*

Francine?

FRANCINE. Francine, is it? Now, it's Francine?!

CONNIE. Come on, honey, give me a break!

FRANCINE. Did you ever give us a break? You and that
phony *(overly pious)* priest!

CONNIE. He was only doing his job.

FRANCINE. If he was so concerned about the Police Depart-
ment why didn't he become a cop!

CONNIE. Boy, are they right what they say about you.

FRANCINE. What did you say?

CONNIE. Nothing! I didn't come here to make trouble.

FRANCINE. How could you, Joe's dead!

CONNIE. And I've come to pay my respects. There's nothing wrong with that. I think it's pretty decent of me, the guy's wife, trying to be nice and you insult me. That's no way to be. Joey is dead. You should learn to let the past rest with him.

(under her breath)

Sometimes…!

*(to **FRANCINE**)*

Where Joey picked you from I'll never know. You know, you should learn to – who gives a shit!

*(**FRANCINE** drops her head.)*

Go ahead, cry your brains out!

FRANCINE. Who's crying?

*(A ruffled **SAMMY** enters from the lobby amid the sound of muffled voices.)*

SAMMY. Francine, can I have a word with you?

FRANCINE. What's wrong?

*(**CONNIE** leans forward to listen.)*

*(to **CONNIE**)*

Do you mind?!

SAMMY. In the private hall.

FRANCINE. Give me a minute.

*(**SAMMY** crosses to the smoking alcove and lights a cigarette while peering out the window. **FRANCINE** stands and **CONNIE** notices she's pregnant.)*

CONNIE. Joey's?

FRANCINE. Who else's?

CONNIE. I mean, I didn't know. Don't get so touchy. Joey never said nothing. A husband doesn't like telling his wife who he's knocked up!

*(The line draws **SAMMY**'s attention.)*

FRANCINE. What?

CONNIE. I don't mean it like that. You got to learn not to jump all the time. I mean…He could have mentioned it. We talk about his car, his mother's varicose veins –

FRANCINE. I didn't know you were so friendly? Excuse me!

(**FRANCINE** *crosses to the smoking alcove,* **CONNIE** *crosses to the casket.*)

SAMMY. *(whispered)* Francine, you okay – feeling okay?

FRANCINE. *(whispered)* I'm fine.

SAMMY. *(whispered)* Joe's wife – she wants to pay for everything.

(**FRANCINE** *glances out at* **CONNIE**.)

FRANCINE. *(whispered)* What did you tell her?

(**CONNIE** *crosses to the plastic gladioli. She tries to sniff them and scratches her nose.*)

CONNIE. Bastards!

SAMMY. You don't need the expense. That's why I didn't want to talk in front of her. If she knew you agreed to pay she might say forget it. She didn't have to ask me for an itemized list! I mean with you, you know, I wouldn't rob you. But strangers, what could you do? They don't trust – it's not worth it. I'm gonna keep this place just for friends!

(**SAMMY** *exits down the private hall while* **FRANCINE** *rushes over to* **CONNIE**.)

FRANCINE. *(to* **CONNIE***)* Did you ask Sammy – Mr. Lucchese for an itemized list of expenses?

CONNIE. So?!

FRANCINE. Who the hell do you think you are?!

CONNIE. Hey, lower your voice – they'll hear ya.

FRANCINE. I don't care who hears me.

CONNIE. I do. The Mayor's out there, with a bishop or a cardinal or some shit. Have some respect.

FRANCINE. For what?! You? Them?!

CONNIE. For nothing! What are you getting so excited about? So I asked a guy how much this shindig is going to cost and you go off the deep end. You better call your doctor, and let him give you something.

FRANCINE. Don't worry, there's nothing wrong with me.

CONNIE. Well, they did put you away.

FRANCINE. I took a rest. If you ever lose a husband, you'll understand.

CONNIE. I just did.

(**CONNIE** *crosses to the front row/second set of folding chairs and parks her purse and veil.*)

I know better not to pay attention to you. Besides everything else, women in your condition – you know – pregnant women!

FRANCINE. Listen –

CONNIE. *(charging over to her)* Listen you! Come on, honey, let's get something straight. I'm trying to give you some advice – take it or leave it. I don't want to see you or nobody go off the deep end, so calm down before you blow a fuse.

(**FRANCINE** *staggers back to the big chair.*)

And as far as that big mouth outside goes – he knows it and you better get used to it. I'm still Mrs. Barbalottio. You know what that means? The bills, right down to the Rosary Beads in Joey's hands, go to me. Me!

FRANCINE. No one asked you to pay for anything, did they?

CONNIE. Then who's going to pay for it? His mother? You got to be kidding – cheap bastard! You? Be my guest! But don't come crying to me when I collect on his insurance.

FRANCINE. Joe didn't have an insurance policy. It was bad luck, like owning a cemetery plot.

CONNIE. Bad luck or not, he had one, and I don't mind telling ya it's a pretty big one to boot. You should learn not to believe everything a man says. Superstition is one thing, stupidity is another. If you don't believe me, call the P.B.A. *(Police Benevolent Association)*; they're making a collection too, and those guys give big! Another type of insurance – you know what I mean? When my brother Jimmy died – God rest his soul – another jerk getting killed for nothing – they got up an awful lot of money. I think you should think twice before dropping ten grand. I mean in your condition. I'm only trying to be fair, honey.

FRANCINE. All that money goes to you?

CONNIE. And my son, Leo – Joey's son! If you're getting any brainstorms you gotta go to court and prove it. You know there are laws…

FRANCINE. Don't worry, I don't want it. Of course you know they don't bring the money here, they mail it to you like on a game show.

CONNIE. You think you're so prim and proper. I know what you're thinking, well, I worked hard for that money.

FRANCINE. It's hard work digging your toes into the sheets every night.

CONNIE. Who the fuck do you think you are?!

FRANCINE. Remember the mayor's outside, and probably sitting with your priest friend.

CONNIE. If you weren't in that condition I'd mop the floors with you. I think you better stop judging other people. You're no saint. You know it's still a sin to sleep with someone else's husband.

FRANCINE. Only on Staten Island!

CONNIE. Staten Island, Brooklyn, the whole world – you'll see. Just look at the people's faces when they come in. Look at the way they look at you and that stomach. As far as I'm concerned you could have your baby right here on the floor. But you gotta be sick to come in here and let people stare at you – real sick.

FRANCINE. I belong here. It's you they'll be looking at – acting like the grieving widow.

CONNIE. I'll act what I want. You know –

FRANCINE. Just leave me alone! I've got three days ahead of me. Let me have them in peace.

CONNIE. Who's stopping ya? If you want to sit here staring at that box, be my guest.

*(**CONNIE** turns to the casket and then quickly back to **FRANCINE**.)*

Let me tell ya something, I knew him just a little bit longer. I'd like to see if this thing happened in ten years with a kid around your neck and him out all night with his stupid friends trying to get a little and the only thing he does home is pick up his weights in the cellar or try to take off you what his girlfriends won't give him in the street!

FRANCINE. Look –

(taking a deep breath)

I'm sorry your relationship didn't work out.

CONNIE. Relationship?! Honey, we were married.

FRANCINE. Call it what you want – we had a different life. For me, Joe was everything I needed. He was always there –

CONNIE. You weren't pregnant long enough!

FRANCINE. I...I'd...I really think –

CONNIE. *(yelling to the casket)* He only lived to run around with his rat-bastard friends!

FRANCINE. Connie, if you don't mind?

CONNIE. A leopard never loses his spots!

*(turning to **FRANCINE**)*

What was he doing on Fifth Avenue?

*(While **FRANCINE** ponders the question, **CONNIE** retrieves her purse and sits in the first row/second set. A moment later the manic **CONNIE** is up and pacing.)*

You don't believe that shit about "special assignment?" Those reporters are dumber than they look. I bet you believe that hero crap too? Good for you. He was the last cop they'd send on a special assignment. Why they never kicked him off the force –

FRANCINE. Thanks to your priest-chaplain friend and his letters about marriage *(that)* he stuffed into Joe's file.

CONNIE. Try graft, honey. They don't kick guys off the force for leaving their wives.

FRANCINE. You threw him out.

CONNIE. Not by a long shot. He had legs – long ones. Nobody pushed him out. He walked and forgot he ever had a family!

(As she fumbles through her purse...)

You got a match? Never mind.

(As she takes a pack of cigarettes and a book of matches out of her purse...)

Believe me, the last thing the Pope needed was Joey for protection.

FRANCINE. They had twelve thousand cops up there.

CONNIE. They could have had twelve million. Joey wasn't supposed to be there. I still got friends in this precinct; Joey belonged in Brooklyn – watching kids cross the street! What a joke. If I know him, he was up seeing one of those – remember a store called "Best" something – Corporation – Company; next to St. Pat's? Remember they tore it down? Everybody made a big stink over it; like who shops on Fifth Avenue anyway?

FRANCINE. I know the store!

CONNIE. Joey used to see a girl – one of the sales –

*(An angry **FRANCINE** jumps up.)*

Oh, I didn't mean anything by it.

FRANCINE. Like hell you didn't!

CONNIE. Relax, honey.

*(**MRS. MARYANNE LONGO** and **MISS PHYLLIS BATTISTA**, two middle-aged Italian-American beauticians enter from the private hall. They wear pink polyester uniforms and "high-style" hairdos and carry big purses, and in **PHYLLIS**' case, also a large over-stuffed totebag. They pause in the smoking alcove.)*

FRANCINE. Stop calling me honey!

CONNIE. Excuse me.

MARYANNE. *(to* **PHYLLIS.***)* Oh, Jesus Christ!

(As **PHYLLIS** *and* **MARYANNE** *cross to* **FRANCINE,** *a resigned* **CONNIE** *reluctantly drops her cigarettes and matches back into her purse then goes and sits back in the front row/second set and lays her purse and veil on the next chair.)*

Francine, I'm so sorry. What a god-damn shame!

(As she kisses **FRANCINE**...*)*

What the hell did he do to deserve this? What a sin – a sin!

(to **PHYLLIS***)*

What was I telling you –

(to **FRANCINE***)*

Only yesterday, that bastard; the joke he played! God forgive me – beautiful man!

(She turns to the casket and then back to **FRANCINE.***)*

You call your doctor? He give you any pills? Anything? You got to take care of yourself.

(Noticing **CONNIE***'s black dress, she turns again to* **FRANCINE**...*)*

You want me to pick you up something black?

(to the casket)

God love him, God love him!

*(***FRANCINE** *tries to get out of her seat, but* **MARYANNE** *pushes her back in it.)*

Don't stand up! We'll –

FRANCINE. I'm alright. I'm okay.

*(***MARYANNE** *and* **PHYLLIS** *deposit their purses and* **PHYLLIS***' big totebag on two chairs in the back row/first set nearest* **FRANCINE.***)*

MARYANNE. Don't mind the way we're dressed; we just ran out of the shop. You know how Nicky is. Wouldn't give us a chance to change.

PHYLLIS. Nicholas is a fanatic for time.

MARYANNE. A real pain in the ass! Oh, you know my friend Phyllis?

PHYLLIS. *(to* **FRANCINE***)* I did your hair once – when Maryanne was in the hospital.

(As **MARYANNE** *crosses to the casket…)*

MARYANNE. When I had my scraping!

FRANCINE. I remember.

PHYLLIS. *(to* **FRANCINE***)* I'm sorry about all this. What could you do? Maryanne told me all about him; made me cry. Such a nice guy! It's true what they say about the "Good."

*(***PHYLLIS** *crosses to the casket and joins* **MARYANNE** *on the kneeler for a quick prayer.)*

MARYANNE. I hate when they're closed. You never know if they're in there.

(Overhearing this makes **FRANCINE** *squeamish; even* **CONNIE** *to some extent.)*

PHYLLIS. Gives me the creeps! He must-a looked pretty bad. Bernard could make you look like Cary Grant after a car accident. When it's closed, God only knows.

(Finished with her prayer, **MARYANNE** *stands, and crosses to the remembrance card table.)*

Get me one with the Holy Family.

MARYANNE. You collect remembrance cards? Well, there ain't any.

FRANCINE. Sammy didn't put them out yet.

*(***MARYANNE** *crosses to* **FRANCINE**. *She makes a hand gesture regarding* **CONNIE***'s presence in the room.)*

Later!

(MARYANNE nods affirmatively and then sits in the folding chair closest to FRANCINE. PHYLLIS finishes her prayers, stands, and crosses to CONNIE.)

PHYLLIS. You're Joe's wife. I'm so sorry.

CONNIE. Thank you very much for coming.

(CONNIE takes her veil and purse off the chair and PHYLLIS sits.)

PHYLLIS. What are neighbors for? I felt so sorry for you last night on the news. All those reporters!

MARYANNE. Phyllis, could I have a word with you?

PHYLLIS. In a minute!

(to CONNIE)

Is Barbara Walters *(TV anchor)* big? I mean —

CONNIE. She's tiny.

PHYLLIS. What about Roger Mudd *(TV anchor)*? He looks short on my screen.

MARYANNE. Phyllis!

PHYLLIS. *(to MARYANNE)* You should have seen it — all those reporters asking her stupid questions like "Did you make your husband macaroni before he went to work?" She didn't know what to say.

(to CONNIE)

I could tell. My mother said the same thing; "What, are they crazy?"

(to FRANCINE)

Another one —

MARYANNE. That's enough!

(She crosses to PHYLLIS and pulls on her arm.)

PHYLLIS. What wrong with you, I'm talking?

MARYANNE. Let's sit down.

PHYLLIS. *(standing)* But —

MARYANNE. I'll explain later. Just go sit.

*(As **PHYLLIS** crosses to the smoking alcove and wanders around, **MARYANNE** crosses to her original seat in the second row.)*

MARYANNE. *(cont.)* *(to **FRANCINE**)* Don't mind her, she means well.

*(And with that, **MARYANNE** gives **PHYLLIS** a dirty look.)*

*(**FRANCINE** and **CONNIE**, in their separate ways, quietly retreat into past memories. **MARYANNE**, with nothing else to do, takes an inventory of the contents in her purse. This gives **PHYLLIS** an opportunity to wander around and examine the room's bric-a-brac. And with that the four depict the various modes of the ancient rite of the wake. Moments later a bored **MARYANNE** tosses everything back in her bag and crosses back to the chair nearest **FRANCINE**.)*

Nicky wanted to come but with all the customers – Saturday and all, well, he feels bad you being a regular and having the luncheonette next door. He told me to tell you if you want your hair done for the funeral he'll open early; all on the arm *(free)*. But you better tell him by Monday!

*(**PHYLLIS** plops down next to **MARYANNE**.)*

PHYLLIS. Sammy really did something with this place. When his father had it, it looked like a hole.

MARYANNE. *(to **FRANCINE**)* Phyllis went to school with Sammy – Twenty-twos down the block.

PHYLLIS. He was a few grades ahead of me.

MARYANNE. Your ass! She almost married Sammy.

PHYLLIS. Maryanne, is that nice? I wouldn't marry him, he gives me the creeps. Even when I lived upstairs I couldn't stand –

FRANCINE. Upstairs – here? I'm across the street all my life…?

PHYLLIS. We moved when I was in high school.

MARYANNE. Nineteen-ten!

PHYLLIS. Maryanne, stop that. It was terrible, people crying in the hall. You couldn't have no parties – nothing.

MARYANNE. *(to* **FRANCINE***)* Don't listen to her. The only reason they moved was Sammy wanted to expand. Lucky she never gave back the key to the hall door – right, Phyllis?

(to **FRANCINE***)*

She's the only sick bastard I know who would keep a key to a place like this!

FRANCINE. *(with a hint of sarcasm)* I was wondering how you got in.

MARYANNE. There are more cops outside than in the whole of Coney Island. You'd think they were giving something away. Some big lug wouldn't let us pass.

PHYLLIS. Even with a key! He said, "What, do you sleep with the dead, sweetheart?"

MARYANNE. I told him to go find the guy who hit Joe, instead of hanging around this dump trying to be seen. Finally told him we worked here. Doing heads!

PHYLLIS. Touching dead people…It gives me the creeps just talking about it.

MARYANNE. Dead people, real people…What's the difference?

(And on that note the three resume their collective mourning and all goes quite again. A moment later, **PHYLLIS** *is looking around the room and makes eye contact with* **CONNIE***.)*

(As **PHYLLIS** *stands,* **MARYANNE** *grabs her.)*

Sit – sit!

(Flustered, **PHYLLIS** *returns to her original seat in the second row, takes out a set of rosary beads, and starts praying.)*

FRANCINE. How's Augie?

MARYANNE. He'll be here later.

FRANCINE. Debbie? She excited about the wedding?

(**MARYANNE** *checks on* **PHYLLIS** *and* **CONNIE** *then turns back to* **FRANCINE**.)

MARYANNE. Francine, she's driving me nuts. She didn't want a veil. Could you believe it?

FRANCINE. Times are changing. Debbie knows how to dress.

MARYANNE. I tried to tell her, you're a good girl! I know my daughter, she's a good girl, and good girls wear veils! Why do you think they stay good?

(**CONNIE** *stands, puts her black veil on her seat. With purse in hand she crosses to the smoking alcove.*)

FRANCINE. *(ref:* **CONNIE***)* Maryanne, some of the biggest "you-know-what's" wear them and walk with their heads high.

MARYANNE. They got to have some face!

(**CONNIE** *recoils, but brushes it off as she lights a cigarette and stares out a window.*)

(**PHYLLIS**, *oblivious to any reference to* **CONNIE**, *turns to* **MARYANNE**…)

PHYLLIS. Maryanne, don't worry about Debbie.

MARYANNE. What?

PHYLLIS. You're getting upset for nothing. She's young.

MARYANNE. Young my ass! I already had two kids by her age, and Augie's mother on top of me.

(to **FRANCINE***)*

I told her, no veil, your father ain't walking you down the aisle – Sara ordered me twelve yards of French Illusion!

FRANCINE. Sara around the corner? I thought she stopped making gowns?

MARYANNE. Not like she used to. I give the old lady a break when she comes in the shop; a little this, a little that. If Nicky only knew I only charge for a cut! She's doing this as a sort of a favor, but I ain't saving nothing! It cost me five hundred dollars for material alone.

FRANCINE. She's a good dressmaker. In Italy she made dresses for royalty. She made my gown.

MARYANNE. I figured your mother went to a store in the City.

FRANCINE. With Sara in the neighborhood – my mother and Sara go back. Down to the last button it was perfect. She even came around the corner and helped me get dressed.

MARYANNE. Phyllis, you shoulda seen her. Francine, you looked like a queen – a real queen. People talked about your dress for weeks, months.

(to **PHYLLIS***)*

She got married the same day, what's her name, Lucy Bird – Lucy Baines Johnson. I remember, my mother and me – God rest her soul – she loved weddings. We watched on television then ran to the church to catch Francine.

(to **FRANCINE***)*

Your dress was a hundred times better. You had it all over her.

*(***PHYLLIS** *puts her rosary back in her purse.)*

PHYLLIS. *(ref: the late Joe)* What a sin. How old was he?

*(***CONNIE** *stands and puts her cigarette out.)*

MARYANNE. I'd say about thirty-five.

(to **FRANCINE***)*

How old was Joe?

(As **CONNIE** *crosses back to her chair in the main room.)*

CONNIE. Forty-one! In November!

MARYANNE. *(to* **CONNIE***)* He looked good for his age – rest his soul. I thought he was younger.

(to **PHYLLIS** *and* **FRANCINE***)*

Looked better than that creep Prince Charles. He goes and has his fun then they make him marry a kid. King or no king, he wouldn't get near my Debbie!

PHYLLIS. They were on the news showing off their new castle.

(to **CONNIE***)*

You should have seen them, but then how could you, being on the news yourself. Life's funny.

*(***CONNIE** *forces a polite smile, then sits. A red rotating police car beacon appears outside the alcove windows, a car door slams, and it's off.)*

You don't know from one day to the next. It gives ya the creeps.

MARYANNE. One day you're walking down the street and the next –

(slapping her hands)

BANG!

*(***MARYANNE***'s words jolt* **FRANCINE***.)*

FRANCINE. What time do you have to be back at the shop?

MARYANNE. Why, you need something, Francine? What is it?

FRANCINE. Nothing, never mind.

(With that **FRANCINE** *crosses to the smoking alcove and paces while massaging the back of her neck.* **MARYANNE** *crosses to her original seat next to* **PHYLLIS***.)*

PHYLLIS. *(whispered)* Is something wrong?

MARYANNE. *(whispered)* I don't know?

*(***BERNARD** *enters from the main lobby amid the sound of many muffled voices. He quietly closes the door behind him and then sneaks up behind* **MARYANNE** *and* **PHYLLIS***.)*

BERNARD. Would the real Marie Antoinette please stand up?

PHYLLIS. Bernard!

BERNARD. Hello Phyllis, what did you use on your head? Spray starch?

PHYLLIS. One of these days…Don't let me start. People like me don't like to talk about people like you, but one of these days I'm going to say something, Bernard.

MARYANNE. Say it. Everybody else does.

BERNARD. Do they ever! How things going, Maryanne?

MARYANNE. Can't kick!

BERNARD. You do Phyllis' hair? Or is it all cotton candy?

(With that **BERNARD** *plays with* **PHYLLIS** *' hair.)*

PHYLLIS. Bernard, stop it! You're going to ruin it with those clammy fingers.

BERNARD. Hitting it with a shovel couldn't ruin it.

MARYANNE. He's just jealous because he can't wear his hair like that.

BERNARD. Please, spare me! So what brings you two here so early? Family, or getting a good seat to see the Pope?

(Gleefully **MARYANNE** *and* **PHYLLIS** *jump up and huddle with* **BERNARD**.*)*

MARYANNE. You think he's going to come?

BERNARD. For Sammy to wear his new suit he must be coming. If you have any old hair hanging around the shop, save it. We can glue it to Sammy's head. That's if Mr. Nicholas doesn't have to bring it home to *Mama*!

MARYANNE. Bernard, he'd kill you if he heard you.

BERNARD. Who? Sammy or the Czarina who runs your shop? The baldest man I've ever met.

PHYLLIS. Don't talk about bald. This morning I had a woman with three hairs on her head. God's my witness, three hairs and she wanted a dye and a set. She needed a hat – that's what she needed. I dyed these three hairs, combed them – pulled them like maybe they would grow. All my work for nothing! Put a two dollar net on and she thought she looked beautiful.

*(***BERNARD, MARYANNE,** *and* **PHYLLIS** *enjoy a laugh. Even* **CONNIE** *laughs, but* **FRANCINE,** *turns and gives* **BERNARD** *a dirty look.)*

BERNARD. *(to* **MARYANNE** *and* **PHYLLIS***)* Ladies, if you will excuse me.

(He crosses to **CONNIE.***)*

Mrs. Barbalottio?

CONNIE. *(extending her hand)* So nice of you to come.

BERNARD. Excuse me, Mrs. Barbalottio, I work here.

CONNIE. *(pulling her hand back.)* I'm sorry.

BERNARD. There is a Mrs. Gutta –

CONNIE. *(putting her veil on)* Already?! Tell them to come in.

BERNARD. I believe she's alone.

CONNIE. Shit!

BERNARD. She's asked to speak to you.

(As he makes a gesture to escort her out, **CONNIE** *bolts up with her purse and storms out through the main door, allowing the sound of the loud hallway banter into the room.)*

(to himself) So if you would follow me?

(The fastidious **BERNARD** *checks the bier area and while doing so studies the lighting. Under* **MARYANNE***'s and* **PHYLLIS***'s watchful eyes he crosses to the dimmer in the smoking alcove and brings up the lights.)*

(Before exiting to the main lobby he turns to **MARYANNE** *and* **PHYLLIS***, and in his best Southern Belle manner, makes a deep curtsey to the floor.)*

PHYLLIS. He's crazy. They got to put him away.

MARYANNE. If somebody doesn't kill him first!

*(***FRANCINE***, while trying to work a cramp in her neck, crosses back to the big chair and sits.)*

Are you alright?

FRANCINE. I probably turned the wrong way or something.

MARYANNE. *(crossing to her)* You want me to massage it?

FRANCINE. It'll go away.

MARYANNE. Did you tell your doctor?

PHYLLIS. It's tension. I get it all the time. Do you have any Valiums? They work like gold – one, two, three!

(MARYANNE massages FRANCINE's neck.)

MARYANNE. Just relax.

FRANCINE. It's okay!

MARYANNE. You'll feel better in a minute.

(PHYLLIS takes a bottle of Valium out of her purse, and crosses to FRANCINE.)

PHYLLIS. If you want a Valium I have them.

MARYANNE. What do you want to do, kill the baby? Get out of here with those junk pills!

PHYLLIS. They're not that strong. Sometimes I take two or three of them –

(to FRANCINE)

They relieve tension.

MARYANNE. Phyllis, let's not make a federal case out of this. She'll be all right in a minute.

PHYLLIS. But –

MARYANNE. But nothing! It's only a pain in the neck like you. Calm down. Maybe you should take one.

(to FRANCINE)

Feel better?

FRANCINE. Much! Thank you.

MARYANNE. Phyllis, lend me a brush!

(PHYLLIS crosses to her totebag, retrieves a bright over-sized comb and hands it to MARYANNE. MARYANNE gives the comb a curious look, then a similar one to PHYLLIS. Ensuring no one is watching, she takes the bobbie pins out of FRANCINE's hair and combs it.)

FRANCINE. You should have been around last night. I thought my neck would break in half.

MARYANNE. Maybe you should call your doctor?

FRANCINE. I did. He told me to take a drink. Would you believe we had none in the house? Dana went down to the bar and made them fill me a glass. She's really funny sometimes.

MARYANNE. Who's Dana?

FRANCINE. Joe's partner.

MARYANNE. The big one?

PHYLLIS. Didn't you get jealous? All day in that car with another woman?

FRANCINE. She's not exactly Angie Dickenson.

PHYLLIS. Even so!

MARYANNE. Phyllis, she's more like Columbo *(TV detective)*. You get what I mean? One time she bumped into me outside the shop, she almost killed me. You think you have a tough time finding a husband.

PHYLLIS. Would you cut it out?

(to **FRANCINE***)*

It bothers her 'cause I'm happy being single.

FRANCINE. You're better off. No attachments. You're better off.

*(***MARYANNE*** stops combing her hair.)*

MARYANNE. Some things are God's will. There's nothing you can do about it.

*(***BERNARD*** enters from the main lobby with a stack of remembrance cards. Upon seeing him,* **MARYANNE** *conceals the comb.* **BERNARD***, paying them no mind, crosses to the remembrance card table and lays the cards out in neat rows. As he works* **FRANCINE***,* **MARYANNE***, and* **PHYLLIS** *continue their conversation.)*

FRANCINE. Carmine died, "It was God's will." A twenty-year-old boy and a senator writes me, "It's God's will!" Lucky he died in sixty-six. At least they made a fuss. By the time Billy around the corner died they were lucky they sent him home.

PHYLLIS. Your husband was killed in Vietnam?

FRANCINE. What husband? We were married two months.

PHYLLIS. That still makes him your husband.

FRANCINE. I suppose so.

(Once the remembrance cards are in their proper order **BERNARD** *crosses to the smoking alcove under* **MARY-ANNE**'*s watchful eyes. As he exits down the private hall* **MARYANNE** *pulls out the hidden comb. While* **MARYANNE** *teases* **FRANCINE**'*s hair into a bouffant,* **PHYLLIS** *crosses to the remembrance card table and selects a few.)*

PHYLLIS. *(ref: the casket's flag)* You must already have one of these, huh?

FRANCINE. I suppose so. If I didn't throw it out.

PHYLLIS. My Aunt Ida has one – when my cousin Chicky was killed in Korea. She puts it out every holiday. Probably worth something today – only has forty-eight stars! Every time she hangs it out, it covers the lady's window downstairs. I tell her, Zia *(aunt)*, fold it in half, but she's crazy. Never listens.

(crossing to her seat)

They should either make them smaller or give people flag poles to go with them.

MARYANNE. You know how big the flagpole has to be to swing a flag that size?

PHYLLIS. You could put it in a garden.

MARYANNE. We're lucky we don't sleep with our asses in the street and you want a garden! Typical of the government – give you something you can't use!

PHYLLIS. Why you would use it after it was on a coffin? Gives you the creeps.

(The plastic floral arrangement catches **PHYLLIS**' *attention.)*

The girls in the shop chipped in with Nicholas to buy a wreath. Something like that, I think.

MARYANNE. Nicky is good like that. Always the first one to shell out.

PHYLLIS. I wanted to order the "Gates of Heaven" or the "Clock," but Maryanne –

(With **FRANCINE***'s hair in place,* **MARYANNE** *hands* **PHYLLIS** *her comb and they both return to their original seats in the second row.)*

MARYANNE. They don't use them anymore!

PHYLLIS. Says who?

MARYANNE. Says me! They're too damn expensive –

(to **FRANCINE***)*

And ugly. The "Clock," the "Chair," the table, the back-house *(outside toilet)* –

(to **PHYLLIS***)*

See where you got to go! They can't even fit them in these new flower cars. What do you think, it's like years ago.

PHYLLIS. Look, Protestant! What do I care about the flower car. People look for those things when they come to a wake. Francine, it's the truth.

FRANCINE. I know.

PHYLLIS. You order the "Bleeding Heart"?

*(***FRANCINE** *nods affirmatively.)*

(standing) See Maryanne, she has taste.

MARYANNE. The "Bleeding Heart," that's different. Husbands, wives –

(to **FRANCINE***)*

You know what I mean? People they *live with* have to send it.

PHYLLIS. *(to* **FRANCINE***)* Roses or carnations?

FRANCINE. Roses! American Beauties, the florist said.

PHYLLIS. That sounds – oh! When my father died, my mother sent the biggest Bleeding Heart – the size of a door. It was the talk of the whole neighborhood. It had the reddest, reddest roses – at least a hundred of them making the shape of the heart. No gladiolas or anything like that. You have to be careful, they like to use them for stuffing. Only babies' breath between the flowers, and then these palm leaves in the back making like a fan. You know how they do it? Lots and lots of ribbons, long ones; each had a little loop like a bow someplace and they all came down the front like tears. When I die that's what I want.

(MARYANNE, in an effort to cheer things up, turns to FRANCINE.)

MARYANNE. She's got to find someone to love her first. Right?!

PHYLLIS. Could you leave me alone? This goes on all day in the shop. Do you need help in the luncheonette?

(FRANCINE crosses to PHYLLIS and gives her a tender hug.)

FRANCINE. You'll have to ask Joaquin. I'm selling it to him – at least I'm supposed to. Now, I don't know. Maybe we'll just be partners. We get along now. We should work well as partners. He's so damn honest – won't go home until the last penny is in the register. He drives me crazy, just like my father used to.

PHYLLIS. See, there's good and bad in all kinds.

FRANCINE. He is good, and his wife; such a nice girl. She called last night. I knew what she was trying to say, but her English...

MARYANNE. It's the thought that counts.

FRANCINE. They're one of the best things that's happened to me. Joe loved them.

PHYLLIS. 'Magine that.

FRANCINE. They're going to ride in the limousine with me on Tuesday; to keep me company. I was going to ask Carmine's mother and father, but with Connie and all, I didn't think – you know what I mean?

MARYANNE. Look Francine, I don't like to butt in, but if you want me to, I'll stay with you just so you have somebody to talk English to.

PHYLLIS. Maryanne, what about Nicholas? He told you no more days.

MARYANNE. Frig Nicholas! I'm entitled to a day off once in a while. If he don't like it there's other shops who'd be pretty happy to get me.

FRANCINE. I appreciate it and all – I don't want you to lose your job. Let's play it by ear. Okay? I have to get some things straightened out with Joe's mother. Last night I called her up, she wouldn't talk to me.

MARYANNE. You should have expected it!

FRANCINE. What I expected was her to act civilized. That's not too much to ask? It's a little late to be holding grudges. I'm going through...

MARYANNE. In situations like this –

FRANCINE. What situation? We weren't doing anything behind anyone's back. I wasn't picked up off the street!

MARYANNE. *(standing)* But you still wasn't his wife! Slice it any way you want.

FRANCINE. What's that have to do with anything?

MARYANNE. A lot! That's what counts now – today, in this room. What do you think Connie and her mother are doing out there? Look, you made the arrangements. It shows the family has some respect for you. So the old lady doesn't talk to you – let it go at that.

FRANCINE. Why should I?!

MARYANNE. Because technically Connie, who is walking around acting like the merry widow, belongs in this chair, not you!

FRANCINE. They haven't lived together in ten years. If I was her, I wouldn't even have shown up. Especially her mother – hated Joe! I should be happy with *some* respect while tramps are given top honors? I think things are a little –

MARYANNE. Forget I even brought it up. Maybe I'm wrong. Things change. You're here, that's all that matters. Not that I want to sound like a prude – I'm not the type, but when things like this happen – I mean, you were living together five years. Just to get the satisfaction of it, you should of married. That's all I'm saying.

FRANCINE. It's not that simple. When Carmine died, so many –

MARYANNE. You were only a kid!

(With that FRANCINE fills with a combination of remorse and rage.)

FRANCINE. Phyllis, you want to know where that flag is – in mothballs with lots of maternity dresses and baby clothes! Tell her Maryanne! I promised never again! And here I am, same room, same flag –

(ref: her pregnancy)

Same everything! The only reason I ever talked to Joe in the first place was because he was bragging about his freedom.

MARYANNE. You wouldn't have gotten married for the baby?

FRANCINE. I don't know. Who knows?

MARYANNE. Did you ask?

FRANCINE. No! Believe me it wasn't that important. When did you know Joe to take anything seriously? When I told him I was going to have a baby, he said if it looked like him, he'd marry me. Then the clown walked around the house all night with a pillow stuffed inside his undershirt. What do you do with him?

MARYANNE. Come on, he loved you.

FRANCINE. I was his audience.

(FRANCINE focuses her attention on the casket and cries softly.)

MARYANNE. Francine, tell Phyllis about the time we went to Coney Island. There was my Augie with his stomach overlapping his belt and Joe – not for nothing, but Joe…Francine, never did I see a man with such a body!

PHYLLIS. Maryanne, that's no way to talk about the dead!

MARYANNE. *(to FRANCINE)* If he wasn't yours…! More than once I wanted to drag him out of that station house by the legs.

PHYLLIS. Augie would break your face if he heard you talking like this.

MARYANNE. Don't let's talk about Augie, he's no saint! I have my cross in life – don't let me talk. Last week, Francine, when we had those few hot days, remember? Your Joe – that bastard – wore those shorts of his; I don't think he ever wore underwear!

FRANCINE. You're terrible!

MARYANNE. I'm human! I got eyes.

PHYLLIS. And a mouth!

MARYANNE. Who am I telling? We're friends here, right or wrong? Phyllis, when you get married you'll understand. Francine, just for curiosity's sake, was he really…

*(**MARYANNE** crosses to **FRANCINE** and whispers in her ear and **FRANCINE** guffaws.)*

PHYLLIS. What are you saying?

MARYANNE. When you're married.

*(to **FRANCINE**)*

Was I right? Nicky said you can always tell by the fingers.

FRANCINE. Nicky? If Joe knew that he'd have gone crazy.

MARYANNE. Don't kid yourself; he knew all he had to know. And not only Nicky, even the guys in the shoemaker used to whistle when he passed. He'd flaunt it, they'd catch it. Men, women – I used to yell after him, "Francine better watch you!" What a beautiful man – real devil!

PHYLLIS. What a shame no one can see him.

MARYANNE. Phyllis!

PHYLLIS. Sorry, I didn't mean anything by it.

FRANCINE. I wish I could see him too.

MARYANNE. It was that bad?

FRANCINE. When I got here it was closed. What was there to see? I'd rather not think about it.

MARYANNE. I'm sorry kid. We won't discuss it. But, you should have asked Sammy – you know…

PHYLLIS. Look, Bernard is good. Even if I can't stand him sometimes. Nobody makes faces up like Bernard. It's a real art.

MARYANNE. *Ancoppa ("Upstairs"),* remember how old she was? Like a young girl he made her look. A miracle! Her daughter kissed his hands. You should have checked into it. People don't like extra work, but if you insist, what can they say. It's your money!

(**FRANCINE** *paces, and as she does, she massages the back of her heck.*)

FRANCINE. It's too late.

MARYANNE. Too late, my ass!

FRANCINE. It's almost two o'clock. People will be coming in – the mayor –

MARYANNE. What are you paying taxes for? Let him wait! Phyllis, go call Sammy!

(**PHYLLIS** *exits down the private hall.* **FRANCINE** *crosses to the casket and kneels. Then she stands and fingers the flag as if it was a blanket and she was tucking Joe in bed. This brings tears.* **MARYANNE** *tries to console her.*)

(**SAMMY** *and* **PHYLLIS** *enter from the private hall. As* **PHYLLIS** *rushes to* **FRANCINE** *and* **MARYANNE,** **SAMMY** *pauses in the smoking alcove to inspect the room's new brightness. As he plays with the dimmer, the irritable* **MARYANNE** *and* **PHYLLIS** *shoot him dirty looks. Once satisfied, he strolls over to* **FRANCINE.**)

SAMMY. *(to* **FRANCINE***)* Something wrong, Francine? Air conditioner too high?

FRANCINE. Sammy, how bad was Joe's face?

SAMMY. What do you mean – were there any marks? Maybe a bruise –

(**FRANCINE** *flinches.*)

(comforting her) That's all!

FRANCINE. *(pulling away)* His head?

SAMMY. His head was fine as far as I could tell.

FRANCINE. But wasn't he –

SAMMY. Shot in the head? No! The newspapers – where they get their information, who knows. It looks good on the front page. It was the back!

(**FRANCINE** *gets a slight muscle spasm in her neck.*)

You all right?

MARYANNE. *(massaging* **FRANCINE***'s neck)* She's all right!

FRANCINE. *(whispered)* Why is the casket closed?

SAMMY. What?

FRANCINE. Why is the casket closed?!

SAMMY. Mrs. Barbalottio, his mother was here –

FRANCINE. What's she got to do with it?

SAMMY. She came in about two-thirty; I was just going home.

(*to* **MARYANNE** *and* **PHYLLIS**)

She wanted to see the deceased. Then said she wanted the casket closed. Sweet little old lady, I'd figured everybody knew what was going on.

(*to* **FRANCINE**)

She stayed about half-an-hour. She took all his belongings and left.

FRANCINE. Why didn't you call me?

SAMMY. Look Francine, I'm not in the business to make trouble. What did she take? A few papers, some clothes? She'll probably give them to you. You can understand my position?

MARYANNE. Francine, let it go.

FRANCINE. No! Open the casket.

SAMMY. There are people outside. How long can I make them wait?

MARYANNE. Until Mrs. Defanie over here is ready to let them in.

SAMMY. *(to* **MARYANNE***)* Be reasonable!

(*to* **FRANCINE**)

I'll do it tomorrow if you really –

FRANCINE. Now! You had no right changing anything before speaking to me.

SAMMY. Francine, please! We're friends and friends –

FRANCINE. This is business, Sammy!

SAMMY. I hate to think about it as that. I took care of your mother, your father – Carmine.

FRANCINE. And I paid you well like you pay me when you sit at my counter. Come on Sammy, you're getting me upset.

(With that, **SAMMY** *masterfully directs* **FRANCINE** *back to big chair and kneels down before her.)*

SAMMY. I don't want to be unpleasant, but last night was last night and today is today. Mrs. Barbalottio, who is the deceased's wife, makes the decisions now. The only reason I didn't say anything to you is because we were friends, but now you're putting me in an embarrassing position.

*(***MARYANNE*** grabs* **SAMMY** *by the arm and pulls him away.)*

MARYANNE. Once word is out on this block you'll be in an embarrassing position! Does Tommy Buttons know you're a worm?

SAMMY. What do you think, you're threatening me? I know he's your brother-in-law.

MARYANNE. Who's threatening you?

SAMMY. Don't be smart, Maryanne!

(to **FRANCINE***)*

See what I mean? These are your friends? They don't know what they're telling you. You're only going to have more aggravation listening to these people.

*(***SAMMY*** pauses to compose himself.)*

Understand my place. Last night I didn't realize the deceased's wife –

PHYLLIS. Stop calling him the deceased! It gives me the creeps!

SAMMY. The late Officer Barbalottio –

PHYLLIS. Sammy!

SAMMY. Phyllis, please!

FRANCINE. Sammy, last night I made arrangements with you. If you can't follow them I'll go someplace else.

SAMMY. You can't do that.

FRANCINE. Phyllis, call Walter B. Cook's!

(PHYLLIS *crosses to her purse to get change for the telephone.*)

SAMMY. That's illegal.

FRANCINE. Try and stop me!

MARYANNE. *(crossing to* SAMMY*)* Her lawyer said "possession is nine-tenths of the law!"

PHYLLIS. What lawyer?

MARYANNE. By the time that little tramp gets around to paying you...

SAMMY. Mind your own business!

PHYLLIS. *(hitting him with her purse)* Mind *your* own business!

(MARYANNE *and* PHYLLIS *close in on* SAMMY *and as they move around him he spins inside their circle.*)

SAMMY. What, do you think I'm playing games around here!

(As MARYANNE *pokes him like a pig with her finger...*)

MARYANNE. Who the hell do you think you're talking to?

SAMMY. If you both don't shut up, I'll throw you out of here!

MARYANNE. Try it!

PHYLLIS. Mister "Big-shot!"

(MARYANNE *grabs* PHYLLIS' *purse and slaps* SAMMY *across the back with it.*)

MARYANNE. "Big shit" is more like it!

SAMMY. Get out! Now!

FRANCINE. *(standing up)* Shut up! Shut up! For what?! For what?! The ten thousand dollars I was paying wasn't enough? You want her money? You'll never get it!

(crossing to **SAMMY***)*

I promise you, you do this to me – to me and Joe – you'll never get a penny from her. If I have to fight her in court until I die.

MARYANNE. Calm down, he doesn't mean it. He'll fix everything.

(to **SAMMY***)*

Tell her you'll fix everything. Tell her!

SAMMY. Francine, I didn't mean –

FRANCINE. Stay away from me!

*(***FRANCINE*** crosses to the casket.* **SAMMY** *follows her.)*

SAMMY. Come now, let me –

FRANCINE. What? Now you're afraid?

MARYANNE. *(trying to console her)* He said he'll do it; let him. It's not worth getting upset.

(As **FRANCINE** *wraps her arms around the casket and cries…)*

FRANCINE. They think it's a game –

MARYANNE. *(crossing to* **FRANCINE***)* Nobody thinks that. Everybody loved Joe.

FRANCINE. A big game, for everyone to see.

MARYANNE. Francine, please…

*(***MARYANNE*** tries to pull her away, but* **FRANCINE** *won't budge.)*

(to **SAMMY***)*

Sammy, go do what you have to. Please!

*(***SAMMY*** removes the table with the remembrance cards, opens the draperies concealing the service elevator, and rings for the elevator.* **FRANCINE** *stands erect and gets another muscle spasm in her neck.)*

You all right now? You want me to rub your neck?

FRANCINE. No. I'm fine.

*(***SAMMY*** crosses to her.)*

SAMMY. Would you like one of us to go to your apartment to get one of Joe's uniforms?

FRANCINE. No uniform. No flags.

SAMMY. But…May I say something?

(*addressing the room*)

Just to keep peace…

FRANCINE. Sammy, Joe was not a hero. Let's not make him look like a hypocrite.

SAMMY. If that's what you want.

FRANCINE. That's what I want. I'll come down and pick out a suit.

(*The sound of the elevator fills the room and they all step back.* **BERNARD** *enters from the elevator.*)

BERNARD. What's going on?

SAMMY. Later!

(**SAMMY** *crosses to the kneeler, as he goes to move it he stops and turns to* **FRANCINE, MARYANNE** *and* **PHYLLIS**.)

Would you wait in the private hall?

(**FRANCINE** *crosses to the smoking alcove, and peers out the window.* **MARYANNE** *first stops at her purse to get some tissues, then crosses to* **FRANCINE** *in the smoking alcove. A wise* **PHYLLIS** *crosses to the smoking alcove and stands in front of* **FRANCINE** *to deliberately block her view of the proceedings.*)

(*As* **BERNARD** *and* **SAMMY** *move the kneeler and the big chair…*)

BERNARD. Would you tell me what's wrong?

SAMMY. (*Ref: the casket*) Help me get this thing out of here.

BERNARD. I knew they wouldn't spring for something they couldn't see. You and your flags!

(*As* **BERNARD** *and* **SAMMY** *glide the casket into the elevator,* **PHYLLIS** *calls out to* **BERNARD**…)

PHYLLIS. Bernard, you better do a good job. I'm counting on you!

SAMMY. They want an open casket.

BERNARD. Do you know how much work it's going to be? I didn't fix him that way!

SAMMY. Just shut up and push!

(*SAMMY and BERNARD exit with the casket.*)

PHYLLIS. *(whispered)* They're gone.

(*PHYLLIS and MARYANNE return to the main room. A sobbing FRANCINE slowly follows after them and MARY-ANNE consoles her.*)

FRANCINE. You think I did the right thing?

MARYANNE. If you wanted it open?

FRANCINE. No – about the suit. I knew Joe wasn't going to work in Manhattan and this happened and I forgot. Now Connie tells me he didn't belong there.

MARYANNE. Are you sure?

FRANCINE. I don't know what to think. But if it is, I don't want any of his friends laughing at him dressed up like a hero.

MARYANNE. Nobody will. Everybody liked Joe – he was too nice for that. Don't worry about nothing. Bernard's another Michaelangelo and Sammy's shit-scared of my brother-in-law Tommy. He'll look beautiful. You did the right thing. And as far as Joe being a hero, he'll always be one in my book. Come on kid, go pick a suit before they go nuts down there.

(*As MARYANNE escorts FRANCINE to the smoking alcove, PHYLLIS crosses to the big chair and picks up FRAN-CINE's purse and sweater. As she picks up the sweater, PHYLLIS spies the NYPD patch and is overwhelmed. She quickly suppresses her emotions and crosses to FRAN-CINE in the smoking alcove. PHYLLIS first hands her the purse, but when handing over the sweater, her manner suggests that she's offering up a religious relic, which FRANCINE registers. They share a private moment as the sweater is passed from one to the other. Under MARY-ANNE's and PHYLLIS' watchful eyes FRANCINE exits*)

*down the private hall. As they cross back to the main
room,* **MARYANNE** *motions* **PHYLLIS** *to help her move the
kneeler out of their path.)*

PHYLLIS. What do you think?

MARYANNE. I don't know? When Carmine died, she had
sort of a nervous breakdown – a miscarriage – everything. She got over it. She's strong.

PHYLLIS. You know Maryanne, you're really something.

MARYANNE. Why? I got feelings!

*(As they place the kneeler in front of the draperies where
the casket stood,* **MARYANNE** *takes notice of the plastic
floral arrangement.)*

Would you look to see who sent that thing? They don't
even wait for you to die, and they're sending flowers.
Everything is fast, fast, fast!

*(**PHYLLIS** crosses to the gladioli floral arrangement.)*

PHYLLIS. They're fake!

MARYANNE. Figures!

PHYLLIS. 'Magine that… You can't tell the fake from the
real. Sooner or later they're going to stop making real
ones.

*(**BERNARD** enters from the private hall carrying a guest
register and slams it down on the stand by the main
lobby doors.)*

MARYANNE. *(to* **BERNARD***)* You know, you really know how
to bust them!

BERNARD. Look, leave me alone.

*(As **MARYANNE** and **PHYLLIS** cross to the big chair in
the hopes of returning it to it's rightful place…)*

MARYANNE. Why don't you make us a cup of coffee? You
got nothing to do 'til she picks out a suit.

*(**BERNARD** crosses to them and grabs the big chair.)*

BERNARD. Contrary to what you might think, this is not a
beauty parlor.

(As he deliberately nudges **MARYANNE** *out of his way with the big chair,* **PHYLLIS** *calls to him…)*

PHYLLIS. "Salon" Bernard, "Salon!" Nicholas says its part of our new image. "Salon!"

(And with that she returns to her original seat. As **BERNARD** *deposits the big chair in its proper place…)*

BERNARD. If he wants a new image he should start by getting rid of you two, and his mother behind the register.

*(***MRS. ROSA GUTTA***, a large intimidating Italian-American woman in her late sixties, dressed all in black, punches through the main door, carrying all the muffled voices in the lobby with her. As* **ROSA** *charges towards the casket area, she wails…)*

ROSA. Joey! Joey!

*(***CONNIE***, storms in and runs after her.)*

CONNIE. Mama! Mama! Calm down!

ROSA. Joey! Joey!

(reaching the kneeler)

Where is he?!

(As **MARYANNE** *plops in the big chair…)*

MARYANNE. He left!

ROSA. *Concetta!* (Tr: Connie!)

*(***CONNIE** *crosses to* **ROSA**.*)*

Che succede qui? (Tr: What is going on?)

CONNIE. I don't know!

(to **BERNARD**)

Where the hell is Mr. Lucchese?!

BERNARD. If you would follow me?

(And once more **CONNIE** *rushes off ahead of him and exits down the private hall.* **BERNARD***, with a nod to* **MARYANNE** *and* **PHYLLIS***, crosses to the main doors and closes them behind him.* **ROSA** *crosses to a folding chair in the front row/second set, turns it towards* **MARYANNE***, and sits. As they share hard glances…)*

(Offstage a clock strikes two o'clock, followed by chimes.)

*(**IT IS SUGGESTED THAT**: since a battle is imminent, Verdi's "Dies irae" be played as the curtain falls.)*

End of Act

ACT TWO

(AT RISE – FIFTEEN MINUTES LATER: The room is the same as we last saw it with the draperies in the casket area left open, revealing the service elevator door.)

*(**MARYANNE** sits in the big chair reading a fashion magazine. **ROSA**, now with her chair facing forward, nervously plays with a roll of Lifesavers. **CONNIE** sits next to **ROSA**. She wears her veil, but not over her face, and occupies her time by scraping the nail polish off her fingertips with her thumb. The only sound heard is that of **ROSA** sucking on a Lifesaver.)*

*(**PHYLLIS** enters from the main lobby, and by the muffled voices accompanying her, we discern that the crowd in the lobby has grown.)*

MARYANNE. *(to **PHYLLIS**)* What did he say?

*(As **PHYLLIS** crosses to her original chair in the back row/first set...)*

PHYLLIS. Another half hour, that's all.

MARYANNE. It would kill him to wash a head once in a while? What time is it?

*(**CONNIE** looks at her wristwatch.)*

PHYLLIS. I don't know. I don't wear a watch.

MARYANNE. Then how the hell are we going to know when our half hour is up?

PHYLLIS. Just feel it; like when you know what time to go home. Just feel it.

MARYANNE. *(standing)* Feel my ass!

CONNIE. *(to **MARYANNE**)* It's two fifteen!

ROSA. *(to **CONNIE**)* *Tenete chiusa la tua bocca! (Tr: Keep your mouth shut!)*

49

CONNIE. Mama, please!

MARYANNE. *(to* **CONNIE***)* Thanks, anyway.

> *(***MARYANNE*** *drops the magazine in* **PHYLLIS***'s lap, and then crosses to the kneeler and while leaning against it peers through the draperies.)*

Phyllis, come here! Pick a husband!

PHYLLIS. What?

MARYANNE. There's got to be at least two hundred eligible bachelors out there.

> *(***PHYLLIS*** *tucks the magazine into her totebag and crosses to* **MARYANNE***. Together they move the kneeler to one side and then both peer out the window.)*

PHYLLIS. *(looking out the window.)* Cops! That's all I need. They all look like bachelors; that's their problem. What do I look like, a dope?

MARYANNE. That one's cute.

PHYLLIS. They're all cute and they all stink. None worth a dime in my book!

ROSA. My son Jimmy was a cop – *Dio benedice la sua anima* – and he was the best husband you could find! *(Tr: God bless his soul)*

> *(***MARYANNE*** *gives her a dirty look and then turns to* **PHYLLIS***.)*

MARYANNE. Don't pay any attention to her.

> *(They turn back to the window.)*

Now look at that one. You can't tell me –

PHYLLIS. That's a fireman. They're a little different.

MARYANNE. Miss "Fuss-pot" finally found something she liked.

ROSA. Look at way they look at men.

> *(***MARYANNE*** *abruptly pulls the draperies closed and turns to* **ROSA***…)*

MARYANNE. Don't start!

> *(to* **CONNIE***)*

MARYANNE. *(cont.)* Hey you, Connie! You better tell her to watch her mouth unless she wants another fight!

CONNIE. Mama please – don't start!

ROSA. *Ma cosa la fa crede, ho paura di loro due? Ho colpito uomini piú grande di loro. Non comincia? Devo sedere in una stanza di puttane!*
(Tr: What do you think I'm afraid of those two? I hit bigger men than that. Don't start? I have to sit in a room with whores.)

PHYLLIS. *(crossing to her chair)* Hey don't call me no *put-tin-a*! I'm a good girl. Clean your own house before you start!

CONNIE. What's that suppose to mean?

*(As **MARYANNE** crosses to the big chair and sits…)*

MARYANNE. Just tell your mother to shut up – that's what it means! Phyllis, did you bring cigarettes?

*(While **PHYLLIS** rummages through her totebag for cigarettes, **CONNIE** takes out her pack.)*

ROSA. *Fumano anche in un luogo come questo?*
(Tr: They even smoke in a place like this?)

*(**CONNIE** throws her cigarettes back in her bag.)*

MARYANNE. Look, I've had enough from you. If you know what's good for you – you keep your mouth shut. You hear me!

PHYLLIS. People in glass houses are always the first ones to throw stones. Here Maryanne. I hope you don't mind a non-filter?

MARYANNE. The way I feel, I'd smoke a cigar.

*(**PHYLLIS** hands **MARYANNE** a cigarette and matches and **MARYANNE** lights up.)*

ROSA. *Non ho mai visto questo nella mia vita. Che é successo alle donne?* – what happened to women?!
(Tr: I never saw the likes of this in my life. What happened to women – what happened to women?)

MARYANNE. *(with cigarette in mouth)* Nothing! We've always been the same. You were just too busy looking at men.

*(**MARYANNE** gets the cigarette stuck to her lip. As she gently removes it she says to **PHYLLIS**...)*

How the hell can you smoke these things?

PHYLLIS. I've been smoking Camels since I was seven. You want me to change now?

*(**MARYANNE** crosses to the smoking alcove to deposit the cigarette in the ashtray and then saunters in front of **ROSA** and **CONNIE** on her way back to the big chair. **PHYLLIS** takes a copy of the Star newspaper [any rag will do] from her totebag and moves to the front row/first set next to the big chair.)*

Maryanne, look at Elvis Presley's daughter. She's so pretty; looks like my niece Nancy.

MARYANNE. Don't bother me with that junk. Two people I hate, Elvis Presley and Jean Harris *(killed a famous diet doctor).* If it wasn't for them, these crap papers would have nothing to write about. And that goes for the Kennedys too. You can't turn a page without seeing one of them wiping their ass.

ROSA. *Anche la famiglia del presidente!*

(Tr: Even the President's family!)

CONNIE. Mama!

MARYANNE. Give me a piece of that paper, before I start boxing a few ears.

*(**PHYLLIS** hands **MARYANNE** a section of the newspaper.)*

PHYLLIS. There's a good story about John Davidson –

MARYANNE. Now I know he's looking for a wife.

*(The eerie sound of the service elevator fills the room. All action stops, and as four sets of apprehensive eyes turn towards the elevator door, they recoil in their seats. **BER-NARD** enters from the elevator. As he holds the elevator door ajar, he glances over to **MARYANNE** and **PHYLLIS** reading the "Star.")*

BERNARD. I see you're taking a culture break.

MARYANNE. She reads this shit!

PHYLLIS. At least it's not "X" rated!

BERNARD. Only mentally! Maid Marion, when you're finished, her royal highness is on the phone.

MARYANNE. *(to* **PHYLLIS.***)* Did you tell Nicky I was taking off Tuesday?

PHYLLIS. Why would I do that?

*(**MARYANNE** gives her a hard look.)*

I told Eva.

*(**MARYANNE** makes a gesture as if to hit her.)*

She asked me!

MARYANNE. How did she ask you?

*(**BERNARD**, in his best manner, steps back to allow **MARYANNE** into the elevator. Peering in, a squeamish **MARYANNE** steps back.)*

Never mind, I'll walk!

*(**BERNARD** exits into the elevator. **MARYANNE** hands **PHYLLIS** her purse and the newspaper then exits down the private hall. As **PHYLLIS** busies herself putting the two sections of the newspaper back together she eavesdrops on **CONNIE** and **ROSA**'s conversation.)*

ROSA. *(to* **CONNIE***)* When that other one comes in, you better tell her about the money.

CONNIE. Don't worry! She don't care about the insurance money, the *busta* – nothing.
(Tr: cash donations or gifts)

ROSA. They never care until they see it slipping through their hands.

CONNIE. I can't keep pestering her!

ROSA. It's your husband. When are you going to grow up?!

CONNIE. Look, I don't want anything on my conscience. You think I like seeing her go crazy?

ROSA. She's not crazy.

CONNIE. What do you think all this stuff? Changing the box, what is that? That ain't crazy? I tell you she's snapping again.

ROSA. It's you that's snapping.

CONNIE. Ma!

(**CONNIE** *catches* **PHYLLIS** *eavesdropping and their eyes lock.*)

PHYLLIS. Would you like a piece of the paper to read while you're waiting?

(**PHYLLIS** *moves a chair closer.*)

There's a wonderful story about famous women's mastectomies.

CONNIE. I have it home, thank you.

(**PHYLLIS** *buries her head in the newspaper, while she continues to eavesdrop.*)

ROSA. When she comes back you tell her your Uncle Johnny stands on one side and who she wants stands on the other (*collecting cash donations*). Fair is fair!

CONNIE. I think it's stupid.

ROSA. Stupid?! You know how much money I gave in my life? Think! I go for twenty every time someone drops dead. You know why? My children – you and your brother, *la buonanima di Jimmy*, and Leo. Think of Leo. Tell me I'm stupid! (*Tr: the late Jimmy*)

CONNIE. You're not stupid.

ROSA. You got to learn the hard way.

CONNIE. Ma, alright! Huh!

(*lowering her voice.*)

I'll tell her when she comes back. Don't get aggravated.

ROSA. Be careful when you talk to her.

CONNIE. Ya know, Ma – I think you're the one that's snapping. I don't even know why I came here. It's not worth the aggravation.

ROSA. You belong here!

CONNIE. Let's drop it, alright. Go call Uncle Johnny, but guaranteed he's the only one collecting money in here.

ROSA. *(as she stands)* When Joey's mother comes, be nice!

CONNIE. What for?

(**ROSA** *drops back into her chair.*)

ROSA. For Leo!

CONNIE. She don't even know he's alive.

ROSA. She's an old lady!

CONNIE. Since when you're so concerned about that old bitch!

ROSA. Connie, watch your mouth.

CONNIE. I really think you're the one snapping.

ROSA. When she dies and Leo gets everything, we see who's crazy.

CONNIE. You forgot about Francine's baby? It's Joey's!

ROSA. She has to prove it in court, and Jenny ain't leaving anything to no moron. That kind of thing is in the blood. But, just in case, you got to be nice.

CONNIE. Ma, go call Uncle Johnny.

ROSA. If he's not there, should I call Cousin Sallyboy? He handled the money when Jimmy died. He's not working, he won't mind being here all day.

CONNIE. Hey, I took three days off when his mother died. Don't let it sound like he's doing me a favor.

ROSA. What are you getting excited about? Sallyboy loves you. You're first cousins!

*(Noticing **PHYLLIS**' continued watchful eyes and ears, **CONNIE** turns to her.)*

CONNIE. Did you read the part about Betty Ford?

*(As **PHYLLIS** fumbles through the newspaper...)*

PHYLLIS. I only have Happy Rockefeller and Shirley Temple. You must have the new issue?

CONNIE. *(to **ROSA**)* Call Sallyboy!

(Three red rotating police car beacons appear outside the smoking alcove windows. A few car door slams, and one by one they slowly drive off as the action inside the room continues.)

ROSA. Uncle Johnny might get mad. Aunt Mary already told him.

CONNIE. Mama, call them both. They can hold hands. One can work for Francine!

ROSA. What's-a-matter with you, you used to be a smart girl. Now you act like you're a groggy idiot.

CONNIE. It's you Ma. You're driving me nuts!

ROSA. You think you're doing me a favor? Do as you please. It ain't my husband, it's yours! I tried to help and what do I get?

CONNIE. Mama, I'm sorry! I'll call!

*(**CONNIE** goes to stand, **ROSA** pulls her back in her seat.)*

ROSA. No, you sit. It don't look right people coming in and you not here.

(ref: the big chair.)

You know that's your chair. People come in they go to that chair.

CONNIE. Mama, would you just do what you have to!

*(**ROSA** stands, and crosses towards the main lobby. **CONNIE** yells after her…)*

Call Annette! See if Leo called?

*(An angry **ROSA** rushes back to her.)*

ROSA. Why don't you call him?!

CONNIE. I can't, you know that.

ROSA. I know nothing! A mother can't call her own son?

CONNIE. Look, you were suppose to wait for him and you come following after me!

*(**MRS. JENNY BARBALOTTIO**, a stately Neapolitan woman in her seventies, enters dressed in classic mourning attire which includes a lace mantilla pinned to her head.)*

(As **ROSA** *crosses to* **JENNY***, she morphs into a grieving, sobbing mother-in-law.)*

ROSA. Jenny! Jenny, I'm so sorry! Just a boy – just a boy! Just like my Jimmy. Oh, God, the crosses we carry.

(A reluctant **CONNIE** *stands.)*

Connie! Connie!

(A seething **CONNIE** *crosses to* **JENNY** *and greets her with an air kiss.)*

CONNIE. Hello, Mom! How do you feel?

JENNY. What's going on? Why ain't they ready? There's people pushing – I was almost knocked to the floor. My legs…As it is they hurt.

(As the three move towards the front of the room…)

ROSA. *(Ref: the big chair.)* Connie, get that big chair for Mrs. Barbalottio.

*(***PHYLLIS** *makes a dash for the big chair and drops her totebag and her and* **MARYANNE***'s purses into it.)*

PHYLLIS. I'm sorry, but this seat is already taken.

*(***ROSA** *escorts* **JENNY** *to the front row/second set.)*

ROSA. *Vieni qui, siedi! (Tr: Here, sit!)*

(As **JENNY** *sits down in the chair closest to the big chair, she gives* **PHYLLIS** *the once over.)*

*(***ROSA** *takes a seat at the far end of the row, and as she does she indicates to* **CONNIE** *to come sit between them.* **CONNIE** *and* **PHYLLIS** *share a knowing glance, and after that, a reluctant* **CONNIE** *elbows in between* **JENNY** *and* **ROSA***. Once the three are settled* **PHYLLIS** *returns to her original seat in the back row/first set.)*

JENNY. *(ref:* **PHYLLIS***) Chi è quella donna?*
(Tr: Who's that woman?)

ROSA. *E' una compagna di quell'altra!*
(Tr: Friends of that other one!)

CONNIE. *(to* **JENNY***)* Mom, can I get you anything?

JENNY. Where is she?

CONNIE. Downstairs picking out a suit!

JENNY. What suit? Who needs a suit?

ROSA. *Stanno per aprire la bara – ha fatto una scenata, e quello scattodi d'un impresario l'ha ascoltaro. Che potrebbe fare, volete lottare con City Hall?!*

(Tr: They're opening the box – she made a scene, and that jerk of an undertaker listened to her. What could you do, fight City Hall?)

JENNY. I told him I wanted it closed.

ROSA. My Connie yelled. But I said we can't afford to make trouble with the people outside – newspapers – it looks bad.

JENNY. And the television – the television! I saw you Connie. All those tears!

ROSA. You saw it? All the neighbors came in this morning after it was on. A lady reporter told my Connie she was as brave as Jackie Kennedy.

JENNY. Like Jackie Kennedy…? And you Rosa, what they say about you?

ROSA. Nothing! They only talked to my Connie.

JENNY. I see, only Connie. They didn't want to talk to Leo? I said "No Leo?", "Where was the son from this *fine family?*"

CONNIE. He was out!

JENNY. Out? His father dead, he was out?

ROSA. He had something to do – important – school work.

JENNY. He must be a smart boy. The school work is more important than a dead father. What about you Connie? You had school work last night? I waited for you. Thinking, "She comes with me to see my son", but no Connie.

ROSA. She got herself so sick we were ready to call a doctor – my poor Connie.

JENNY. Only mothers can't get sick. Especially when their hearts are ripped apart!

CONNIE. I'm sorry Mom, but I couldn't come. Everything was happening at the same time. How come you picked this place – it's so far.

JENNY. She picked it. At least she called.

ROSA. My Connie wanted to, but the reporters –

JENNY. And the doctors! Connie, why don't you take off that veil? You look just a little too sad.

(**CONNIE** *rips the veil off her head and dumps it in* **ROSA***'s lap. And with that she crosses her arms and fumes!* **ROSA** *takes out a hair brush and tries to hand it to* **CONNIE**.)

ROSA. Here, Connie!

(**CONNIE** *refuses it!* **ROSA** *turns to* **JENNY**.)

E' troppo disturbata perchè quell'altra sta qui. Neanche si pre-occupa di sua figura. Povera mia Concetta.

(Tr: She's just so upset by that other one being here, she doesn't even care about how she looks. My poor Connie.)

JENNY. *Povera Concetta!*

(Tr: Poor Connie!)

CONNIE. I'll be right back. I need a cigarette!

(**CONNIE,** *with purse in hand, charges out to the main lobby and is greeted by raised voices.* **JENNY** *stiffens up under* **ROSA***'s watchful stare. After a long pause,* **JENNY** *stands and crosses towards the gladioli floral arrangement. As she walks she keeps a close watch on* **PHYLLIS***, who in turn keeps a close watch on her, and the big chair.)*

JENNY. Nice flowers. Big!

ROSA. They're plastic!

(Repelled, **JENNY** *returns to her seat next to* **ROSA**.)

JENNY. What's this world coming to? Every day something different! Rosa, where's Leo? I didn't see him outside. I called the house to make sure you know where to go. When I ask for Leo, your sister Annette tells me she don't know where he is!

ROSA. We didn't want him to come.

JENNY. He belongs here!

ROSA. But not now with that other one here! It don't look right for the boy. What did we do to deserve this disgrace? If the reporters find out – do you know the Pope might come back just to say Joey's mass? God only knows who he's going to take from Washington. Forget St. Patrick's when this comes out. We all look bad, even Joey – *Dio benedice la sua anima* – all because of that – don't even let me say it. *(Tr: God rest his soul!)*

JENNY. Connie, she talk to her?

ROSA. Connie tried. She talks stupid.

JENNY. "Stupid?" *Che è questo, "stupido?"*
    (Tr: What is this "stupid?")

ROSA. They put her away once. Who knows where; maybe Kings Park! *(a Long Island hospital for the insane)*

JENNY. My Joey, what was he doing? He's better off dead. What got into that boy?

ROSA. Maybe you can say something to her. We don't want her to leave. Let her stay, but she don't have to sit on top of him. Come on, what is this? Girls like that know their place. That chair is my Connie's!

JENNY. We see. We see.

ROSA. If she had a family, but even they don't want to know her.

    *(**FRANCINE** enter from the private hall with her purse and sweater. **MARYANNE** is with her. They pause in the smoking alcove.)*

MARYANNE. *(whispered)* Is that his mother?

FRANCINE. *(whispered)* I don't know. I think so.

    *(**ROSA** spots **MARYANNE** and **FRANCINE** and turns to **JENNY**...)*

ROSA. *Ecco la troia! (Here's the tramp now!)*

    *(**JENNY** turns towards the front door.)*

    (pointing to the alcove)

    Sta venendo! (Tr: Over there!)

JENNY. *(ref:* **MARYANNE***) Quella donna vecchia?!*
  (Tr: That old woman?!)

ROSA. The other one!

JENNY. *(ref:* **FRANCINE***'s pregnancy) Madre di Dio!*
  (Tr: Mother of God!)

ROSA. You didn't know?

JENNY. Know? What is this?!

MARYANNE. *(whispered)* Just be polite. It can't hurt. You get more with sugar.

  (As **FRANCINE** *crosses to* **JENNY,** **JENNY** *stands.)*

JENNY. What is this? What are you doing? That's not my son's! You got yourself in trouble; don't come round my door. I know about women like you!

  *(***MARYANNE** *grabs* **FRANCINE***'s arm and escorts her to the big chair.)*

MARYANNE. Let's sit down. Don't pay attention to her.

FRANCINE. Wait a minute, Maryanne.

MARYANNE. Come on, you don't need this!

  *(***MARYANNE** *shoves* **FRANCINE** *in the big chair and pulls a chair from the front row/first set, bangs it down next to the big chair and sits in it.)*

JENNY. *(sitting next to* **ROSA***)* And you knew?

ROSA. Me? We just found out!

  (And with that **ROSA** *and* **JENNY** *fume and fume.)*

  *(***CONNIE** *enters and quietly takes a seat behind her mother.)*

  *(***JENNY,** *while looking straight ahead address* **CONNIE** *behind her…)*

JENNY. You knew about *"La Bellezza?"* *(Tr: "The Beauty")*

CONNIE. Who knew?

JENNY. What are you going to do about it?

CONNIE. Nothing! What can I do?

JENNY. *(turning to* **CONNIE***)* If it was my husband…!

*(As an enraged **JENNY** turns to **FRANCINE**, an incensed **CONNIE** dismisses her with a wave of her hand.)*

JENNY. *(cont.)* Hey you! I want to talk to you.

MARYANNE. *(to **FRANCINE**)* Let her come over here!

FRANCINE. It's okay.

MARYANNE. It's not okay. Sit!

FRANCINE. *(to **JENNY**)* Yes! What is it?

JENNY. Why you open the box?

FRANCINE. Why did you close it?

JENNY. Where you live, across the street? I live on Long Island. You know it takes me two hours to get here last night – two hours with arthritis in my legs – lucky I got good neighbors – two hours just to see my poor beautiful son. You couldn't come across a street?

FRANCINE. There was no need.

JENNY. No need? Now you know why the box was closed.

PHYLLIS. *(to **MARYANNE**)* Boy, that's the cruelest thing I ever heard!

JENNY. I'm cruel? *"La Bellezza,"* she kills two healthy men. I'm cruel? *Strega!*
(Tr: "The beauty") (Tr: Witch)

MARYANNE. Francine, don't listen to her!

JENNY. How many more sons? The first mother should have killed you!

MARYANNE. *(to **FRANCINE**)* It's not your fault!

JENNY. *Strega, strega!* How many more sons?! *(Tr: Witch, Witch!)*

MARYANNE. *(to **FRANCINE**)* She don't know what she's saying.

JENNY. How many?!

*(**MARYANNE** bolts from her seat.)*

MARYANNE. All right, that's enough!

JENNY. Who are you? Where do you belong? Get out of here!

MARYANNE. What the hell is wrong with you; picking on her for no reason at all? Sick bastards, all of you!

FRANCINE. Maryanne, please!

*(A tense **FRANCINE** leans forward and massages the back of her neck.)*

JENNY. *(Ref: **MARYANNE**) Figlia di merda!*
(Tr: Daughter of shit!)

MARYANNE. Somebody better keep that old woman's trap shut if they know what's good for her!

CONNIE. Mom, please! Mama, tell her!

ROSA. *Jenny, sta zitto!* It's no good to argue with them.
(Tr: Jenny, keep quiet!)

JENNY. And I should let this *puttana* – *(Tr: whore)*

*(**CONNIE** jumps up and so does **PHYLLIS**!)*

– say what she wants to me. You want me to be quiet?

MARYANNE. Watch who you're calling a whore! Old or not, I'll wipe the streets with you!

*(As **MARYANNE** makes a move towards **JENNY**, **FRANCINE** jumps in front of her and charges over to **JENNY**.)*

FRANCINE. *(to **JENNY**)* Stop it! Stop it!!!

*(**FRANCINE** raises her hands in anger, catches herself, and pulls back so fiercely it causes a severe cramp in her neck. As she leans forward and places her hands around the back of her neck the pain freezes her in place.)*

MARYANNE. Francine! Francine! Oh my God!

*(**MARYANNE** rushes towards **FRANCINE**.)*

CONNIE. Don't move her!

*(**CONNIE** flies around **ROSA** and **JENNY** and takes hold of **FRANCINE** from behind and carefully wraps her arms around her waist.)*

Where does it hurt?

*(As **CONNIE** leans into her, she rocks her back and forth and soon a relaxing **FRANCINE** picks up the rhythm and they become one.)*

ROSA. *(irritated)* Connie!

CONNIE. Ma! Huh!

> *(to* **FRANCINE***)*

> You feel any pain in your stomach?

> **(CONNIE** *helps* **FRANCINE** *to the big chair and then goes behind her, gently removes* **FRANCINE***'s hands from her neck and replaces her own and begins neck massage.)*

JENNY. Help her! *Aiutala a morire!* Keep helping her, maybe you die too! *(Tr: Help her to die!)*

ROSA. *(standing)* Hey, you're talking about my daughter!

JENNY. Your daughter – where was she last night?

CONNIE. What business is it of yours?!

> *(to* **FRANCINE***)*

> Just relax.

JENNY. Where were you?

ROSA. Connie, don't pay any attention to her!

CONNIE. *(to* **FRANCINE***)* Just relax.

FRANCINE. *(sobbing)* She has no right. No right!

CONNIE. Just relax honey, it's not worth it!

> *(to* **MARYANNE** *and* **PHYLLIS***)*

> Maybe a cold rag!

MARYANNE. I'll get it.

> **(MARYANNE** *exits down the private hall.)*

JENNY. One worse than the other!

> *(As* **CONNIE** *gently massages* **FRANCINE***'s neck she turns to* **JENNY**…*)*

CONNIE. Look, I'm tired of your remarks. Where was I last night? Well, wherever I was, I wasn't coming here! You think you're spiting anyone by not letting us see your precious son? I was glad the damn box was closed!

> **(FRANCINE** *flinches.)*

> *(to* **FRANCINE***)*

CONNIE. *(cont.)* Am I hurting you, honey?

(to **JENNY***)*

You think I like being here? Well believe me, being in a room with you and your son – dead or alive – stinks!

ROSA. Connie!

CONNIE. Ma, please! I'm fed up. Up to here! She thinks a saint died. Saint my ass!

ROSA. Connie, for me! Please! You'll regret it later. Please!

*(***MARYANNE** *enters from the private hall carrying a damp cloth, crosses to* **CONNIE** *and hands it to her.)*

JENNY. *Lascia parlare – lascia parlare! (Tr: Let her talk, let her talk!)*

(While **CONNIE** *applies the damp cloth on* **FRANCINE** *'s neck…)*

CONNIE. You're damn right I'll talk! –

MARYANNE. *(to* **FRANCINE***)* – You all right?

CONNIE. – Seventeen years I've had to hear your bullshit! I thought once he left – once I kicked him out! I thought I heard the last of you, but no, you never let up.

*(***SAMMY** *enters from the private hall carrying a paper cup filled with whiskey. He crosses to* **FRANCINE***.)*

The most aggravating bastard!

SAMMY. *(to* **FRANCINE***)* – Here, drink this!

JENNY. *(to* **CONNIE***)* "Aggravate!" "Aggravate!" A guilty conscience makes you aggravate!

FRANCINE. *(to* **SAMMY***)* – What is it?

CONNIE. *(to* **JENNY***)* My conscience is clear. I was too good wife! –

*(***SAMMY** *hands the paper cup with whiskey to* **MARYANNE. MARYANNE** *helps* **FRANCINE** *drink it.)*

SAMMY. *(to* **FRANCINE***)* Drink it, it's just whiskey to calm you down. You want me to call your doctor?

CONNIE. *(to* **JENNY***)* – Too good for the likes of your son!

FRANCINE. *(to* **SAMMY***)* No! There's nothing wrong.

CONNIE. *(to* **FRANCINE***)* Listen honey, he might have been good to you but as far as I was concerned he was a first class louse with a capital "L"!

JENNY. And what were you? Fooling around with other men! Don't let me talk.

CONNIE. Hey, talk, what I do with my life is none of your damn business.

ROSA. *(to* **JENNY***)* Connie was a good wife! The best mother!

JENNY. Rosa, take your daughter out of here before I say something we'll all regret.

*(***ROSA*** slowly rises from her seat with the power of a volcano ready to erupt.)*

ROSA. Jenny, I've been nice. Enough is enough!

*(***JENNY*** fearlessly stands and she and* **ROSA** *face off.)*

PHYLLIS. *(to* **SAMMY***)* You better do something!

ROSA. *(to* **JENNY***) Scusami, con rispetto di tua età, dunque metti piedi dentro il mio terreno. Capisci? (Tr: Excuse me, with respect for your age, but you're overstepping your boundaries. You understand?)*

SAMMY. Ladies! Maybe you'd like to step outside for a breath of fresh air? We have a few minutes before we will be ready. Maybe you'd like to freshen up. There are two ladies rooms; one on this floor and one downstairs.

PHYLLIS. That sounds nice. I'd like a glass of water – anyone else?! Francine?

FRANCINE. That sounds nice.

*(***SAMMY*** makes a hand gesture to* **CONNIE** *indicating trouble brewing between* **JENNY** *and* **ROSA**…*)*

SAMMY. *(to everyone)* Maybe some air?!

CONNIE. *(crossing to* **ROSA***)* Mama, come on! Let's go out!

ROSA. No, I'll stay here!

JENNY. Go! I'll watch the money for you.

ROSA. What's that supposed to mean?

JENNY. Do I look stupid?

ROSA. *Quale moneta guarderá? Non guarda la moneta da la tua famiglia?* The cheapest bastards on earth – your people! They don't have a pot to – *(Tr: What money you going to watch? Not the money from your people?)*

SAMMY. Ladies, please! There are people out there.

(CONNIE grabs ROSA forcefully and together they head towards the main exit. JENNY sits. MARYANNE takes the damp cloth off FRANCINE's neck and the paper cup from her hand and crosses to the smoking alcove. PHYLLIS gently helps FRANCINE from her chair and they cross towards the smoking alcove. SAMMY rushes ahead of CONNIE and ROSA to open the doors, but CONNIE reverses back to fetch their purses. As CONNIE leans forward to take ROSA's purse off the chair next to JENNY, JENNY sighs...)

JENNY. My son, my poor son had to carry this cross!

CONNIE. The only cross your son carried was you!

(JENNY lunges at CONNIE! A shrieking ROSA storms through the folding chairs toppling them this way and that; creating havoc in her wake. As she nears JENNY, JENNY too shrieks with rage. CONNIE bolts between the two of them, pushing JENNY off while trying to hold ROSA back.)

Mama, please, Mama!!!

PHYLLIS. Oh my God! Maryanne!

MARYANNE. Let them kill themselves!

(FRANCINE rushes to CONNIE's aid and tries to separate the three.)

Francine!

(In a flash, MARYANNE and PHYLLIS charge in and try to break up the fight. Before long all six are screaming! CONNIE grabs the feisty ROSA's wrists and tries to push

her back. **MARYANNE** *blocks a frantic* **FRANCINE** *from harm.* **PHYLLIS** *grabs the wiry* **JENNY** *from behind and backs her away. And like a referee, the frantic and inept* **SAMMY** *makes circles around them.)*

*(***BERNARD*** *enters from the private hall with his shirt sleeves rolled up and wearing bright rubber gloves.)*

BERNARD. What the hell is going on in here?!

(As he separates them, his rubber-gloved hands do not go unnoticed and act as a repellent reminder of where they are and they back off.)

Please, control yourselves!

(As he picks up the fallen folding chairs he yells to **SAMMY** *…)*

Where the hell are the men in this family? You know better to let women in here alone!

(to the ladies)

Now sit down or get out!

*(***SAMMY*** *and* **BERNARD** *put the folding chairs back in their original places, while the women pick their belongings off the floor.* **MARYANNE** *and* **PHYLLIS** *help* **FRANCINE** *into the big chair and then go to their original seats in the second row/first set.* **BERNARD** *crosses to the second set and forcefully indicates to* **CONNIE, ROSA** *and* **JENNY** *that they should occupy the front row. Now spent,* **JENNY** *and* **ROSA** *take the two end chairs, which forces* **CONNIE** *to sit between them.* **MARYANNE** *looks over at the three, then quietly moves to the front row in the chair closest to* **FRANCINE. MARYANNE,** *the sentinel, looks over at* **JENNY** *and she returns* **MARYANNE***'s stare.)*

CONNIE. *(whispered)* Mama, please – your blood pressure. Please, Mama, for me. Please!

(As **BERNARD** *places the last of the folding chairs back in place…)*

BERNARD. I got work to do and I have to referee tag teams?

(to **SAMMY***)*

If this happens again –

(turning to the ladies)

– Common nobodies!

SAMMY. *(slapping* **BERNARD***'s arm)* Hey!

BERNARD. *(crossing to the smoking alcove)* Next year the City. I don't care how little they want to pay. It can't be worse than this!

*(***SAMMY** *goes after him and grabs him.)*

SAMMY. *(whispered)* Hey! What the hell are you doing?

BERNARD. *(whispered)* Don't! Just leave me alone!

SAMMY. *(whispered)* Keep talking to people like that –

BERNARD. Then you go down stairs and fix him up!

(Before exiting down the private hall, a spited **BERNARD** *pushes the dimmer all the way up, which causes the room to be flooded with harsh light and startles the women who either jump or holler.)*

SAMMY. *(whispered)* Son-of-a-bitch!

(As **SAMMY** *stands guard, he slowly lowers the lights to their original setting and the women calm down.)*

ROSA. *(under her breath) Male...Il diavolo!*
(Tr: Bad...The devil!)

CONNIE. Mama!

ROSA. *(to* **JENNY***) Tu sei come un diavolo!*
(Tr: You are like the devil!)

CONNIE. Mama!

JENNY. See... See what it is to lose a son. Wait, then you see.

CONNIE. Do you know what you're saying? You're talking about your own grandson, your own blood, when you talk about Leo. "Lose a son?" Mama, tell her who lost a son.

ROSA. You don't have to let anyone know your business.

CONNIE. It's her business, like it's yours and mine.

(to **JENNY.***)*

You know why Leo isn't here?

ROSA. Connie, no!

CONNIE. Leo ran away!

JENNY. Living in a crazy house, no wonder!

ROSA. I took care of Leo like he was my own son!

JENNY. Then it's my fault?

CONNIE. Nobody is blaming anyone.

JENNY. Sixteen year-old boys run away. They come back.

CONNIE. Mom, he ran away with a man. You know what that means?

ROSA. *(to* **JENNY***)* He's confused, he's going through –

CONNIE. Mama!

(to **JENNY***)*

Leo is queer.

ROSA. Connie!

CONNIE. I don't care who knows it – even the reporters!

ROSA. *(to* **JENNY***)* She did nothing wrong!

> (**CONNIE** *cries and* **ROSA** *comforts her in her big motherly arms.* **MARYANNE,** *overwhelmed by* **CONNIE** *and* **ROSA***'s mother/daughter moment, reaches in her purse for a tissue. As she blows her nose, she turns to* **PHYLLIS…***)*

MARYANNE. I think we better get back! Francine, why don't you get out of here? This is no good for you. These kind of things destroy your insides. For the baby, come on!

FRANCINE. *(standing)* I'll walk you out.

> (**PHYLLIS** *grabs her things and crosses to* **CONNIE.***)*

MARYANNE. *(exasperated)* She has to make the rounds?!

> *(Realizing* **CONNIE** *is too upset to look up at her,* **PHYLLIS** *turns to* **MARYANNE** *and makes a gesture that says,*

*"perhaps later!" The offstage chimes ring three o'clock.
As* **FRANCINE, MARYANNE,** *and* **PHYLLIS** *cross to the
main exit* **SAMMY** *goes after them.)*

SAMMY. Come this way! The front's jammed!

(As they head towards the smoking alcove, **FRANCINE**
takes **PHYLLIS** *' arm.)*

FRANCINE. I don't know what I would have done without
you. When this is over, come to the luncheonette one
afternoon. We can have some coffee.

*(****FRANCINE**** and* **PHYLLIS** *cross to the smoking alcove
and exit down the private hall. Before* **MARYANNE** *can
follow,* **SAMMY** *corners her.)*

SAMMY. And don't forget to tell your brother-in-law Tommy
what I did for you.

MARYANNE. *(brushing him aside)* Don't worry!

*(And with that she saunters down the private hall leav-
ing* **SAMMY** *in the smoking alcove to keep watch over the
other three.* **CONNIE,** *now feeling stronger, takes a pack
of cigarettes out of her purse.)*

ROSA. Connie, not in here!

JENNY. Leave her be!

*(****CONNIE**** pries herself away from them and joins* **SAMMY**
in the smoking alcove.)

SAMMY. *(whispered)* They all right?!

CONNIE. *(whispered)* Don't worry.

*(****SAMMY**** lights her cigarette.)*

Thanks!

*(****SAMMY**** exits down the private hall. Deep in thought,*
CONNIE *paces as she puffs away.)*

*(****JENNY**** stands and crosses to the remembrance card table.
While examining the cards bearing her son's name, she
calls to* **CONNIE**...*)*

JENNY. How long is he gone?

ROSA. A week, the most!

JENNY. You tell my Joey?

CONNIE. What could he do? Leo's not a baby anymore. And when things go wrong, Joey only knows how to hit. It would have made it worse.

JENNY. We call the police. They bring him back. They should hang these men like rats!

CONNIE. Mom, you don't understand –

(Crushing her cigarette in an ashtray, CONNIE crosses to her.)

He has to come back on his own. He's embarrassed. I caught him.

ROSA. Boys do these things.

CONNIE. Come on Mama, this has been going on for years. If I could have turned my back this time, I would have. It was too late He's just like his father; too dumb to hide his mistakes.

(JENNY picks a few remembrance cards off the table, and as she flashes them at CONNIE like a hand of playing cards…)

JENNY. Does he know his father's dead?

(As CONNIE and ROSA share a knowing glance, she replies to JENNY.)

CONNIE. He knows. I don't know what it's going to do to him. He comes, he don't. I can't be in two places –

ROSA. *(standing)* He walks in here and finds that other one with the stomach – in *your* chair!

(crossing to JENNY)

Tell her Jenny! What is he going to think?

CONNIE. Mama, could we stop with that!

JENNY. Connie, listen to your mother.

ROSA. *(to JENNY) Allora, cosa fai? Dimmelo?*
    (Tr: So what do you do? Tell Me?)

CONNIE. Mama, she's a sick girl!

ROSA. *(to* **CONNIE***)* She's not even wearing black!

CONNIE. She's having a baby. Don't make it worse for her. Please, for my sake.

*(***CONNIE*** crosses to the casket's empty space and* **ROSA** *follows close behind.)*

ROSA. Me? I don't let anyone feel bad. But what are you going to tell those reporters when they ask why you sit in the back of St. Patrick's when that *puttana* sits in the front row? I don't care, I'm an old woman. How much more do I have? God only knows, but you Connie, your Leo… With God's help, you will both live a long time, and I tell you, people – they talk a long, long time. Sometimes they never stop! *(Tr: Whore)*

CONNIE. Ma, please, I'm here. That's bad enough!

*(***JENNY*** slams the remembrance card down on the table in a manner reserved for losing hands of cards.)*

(to **JENNY***)*

It's not the way it sounds. Joey and me…In a few years when he got this all out of his system maybe things would be different, but now…Well…I think it's unfair to cause her trouble.

JENNY. The only thing that is fair is what's good for your son. Your son must always come first. Always!

ROSA. *(to* **CONNIE***)* We don't want to throw her out.

JENNY. Yes, she must go. Only one wife, that's it!

CONNIE. No!

(As **JENNY** *crosses to the plastic gladioli floral arrangement…)*

JENNY. I rather die than have a *malafigura*. Only one wife for the priest, the television – for everything! *(Tr: Bad showing)*

(As **JENNY** *inspects the plastic gladioli…)*

They even smell like flowers. How do they do these things?

(turning to **CONNIE***)*

JENNY. *(cont.)* Your Leo must know that his grandmammas love each other, and they love his mother and they love him. When he knows this love, he'll come around. You see!

(Turning to **ROSA** *and speaking with a twisted hand gesture she says...)*

And the other thing –

(Using a turning of a knob hand gesture...)

Ripariamo! (Tr: We fix)

(JENNY *takes an envelope out of her purse, crosses to* **CONNIE** *and hands it to her.)*

My Joey – you want to know why he's in front of that church?! He no works – he sees a lawyer. Look at the papers.

(CONNIE *opens the envelope and finds divorce papers stuffed inside with a greeting card addressed to* **FRANCINE_.***)*

Divorce papers; in a pretty card for her.

(to **ROSA***)*

They were in his jacket.

(ROSA *crosses to* **CONNIE** *and tries to glimpse the divorce papers, but* **CONNIE** *prevents her.)*

(As **JENNY** *crosses to the smoking alcove she talks to* **CONNIE** *over her shoulder...)*

You want to be nice to her? How nice is she to you?

ROSA. *(stunned)* Divorce! Divorce! If this gets out, Leo will never come home. Never!

JENNY. Don't worry. I called the lawyer. As long as he gets his thousand dollars, he won't talk to no reporters.

(Once in the alcove, she turns on her heels and makes a balancing scale gesture with her arms.)

What do I do? I got one grandson and a mother this way, and one –

(Like a beast **ROSA** *charges at her.)*

ROSA. You only have one grandson, Leo! I told you she's crazy. God knows it, it's a pillow! She's doing this to laugh at you.

JENNY. Nobody laughs at me. Nobody!

*(***ROSA*** *crosses to the big chair and motions* **CONNIE** *to sit in it.)*

ROSA. Connie, for Leo!

*(***CONNIE*** *and* **ROSA** *share a knowing glance.)*

I'll put her things on the side.

(With that **ROSA** *takes* **FRANCINE**'s *sweater and purse from the big chair. As she crosses to the back row/second set she spies the NYPD patch on the sweater and unfolds its manly size and waves it before* **CONNIE**. *As a defeated* **CONNIE** *crosses to the big chair and sits,* **ROSA** *dumps the sweater and* **FRANCINE**'s *purse onto one of the back row/second set chairs as if they were trash.* **ROSA** *takes the black veil, stands behind her and places it on* **CON-NIE**'s *head as if it were a crown.)*

(As **ROSA** *adds the final touch – lowering it over* **CON-NIE**'s *face,* **CONNIE** *bows her head in shame.)*

Connie these kinds of women, they trick men.

*(***ROSA*** *then motions* **JENNY** *to sit and* **JENNY** *takes a seat at the far end of the front row/first set. Then with a sense of accomplishment,* **ROSA** *takes the seat closest to her daughter.)*

JENNY. When she comes in I'll talk to her. We won't talk lawyers, divorce, nothing!

(A euphoric **ROSA** *nods, affirmative. And with that the three women sit in silence staring down at the space Joe's body is soon to occupy. A few moments later a flustered* **CONNIE** *sits up and folds the veil back off her face.)*

CONNIE. *(to* **ROSA***)* You happy?

ROSA. What are you talking about?

(As **CONNIE** *slams her hand down on the arm of the big chair…)*

CONNIE. This!

(Waving the divorce papers in **ROSA***'s face…)*

And this!

ROSA. I'm your mother. I only want for *you*!

CONNIE. *(with rage)* That bastard is better off dead!

*(***JENNY** *looks away pretending she didn't hear* **CONNIE***'s outburst.)*

ROSA. Connie, not now!

(With great frustration **CONNIE** *cries out…)*

CONNIE. *When?!*

*(***FRANCINE** *enters from the private hall. Stunned to find* **CONNIE** *sitting in her chair and* **JENNY** *and* **ROSA** *sitting beside her like armed soldiers, she pauses and weighs the situation. With a burst of energy she crosses to the chair holding her belongings and gathers them up into her arms.)*

FRANCINE. *(yelling to them)* Sit where you want. Sit in the damn casket for all I care!

*(***JENNY***, with her back to* **FRANCINE***, calls out…)*

JENNY. That's all you care is to take husbands!

(This causes **FRANCINE** *to charge over to her.)*

FRANCINE. I met Joe three years after he was out of her house. Three years!

(With that **FRANCINE** *crosses to the front row/second set and finds a seat.* **JENNY***, while looking straight ahead, calls to her…)*

JENNY. That luncheonette, where is it? Across from the what – Police Station?! How many years were you there? How many years was my Joey in the Police Station? Do I look like a fool?

FRANCINE. No! I look like a fool for trying to reason with you. You got your chair, that's what you want, now please leave me alone.

JENNY. *(turning to* **FRANCINE***)* Last night I said to myself, so a few people talk. Joey was a man and men do these things.

(As she stands and crosses to **FRANCINE**…*)*

But today, with them two on the television and you with the belly – now, even the Pope! *Madre Di Dio,* what is this going to turn into? *(Tr: Mother of God)*

FRANCINE. *(to* **CONNIE***)* Please, could you –

JENNY. It's got to stop!

FRANCINE. Connie, could you call her off?

*(***FRANCINE***,* **JENNY** *and* **ROSA** *turn towards* **CONNIE***, but all* **CONNIE** *does is look down at the divorce papers.)*

JENNY. You got to leave!

FRANCINE. What, are you crazy? If anyone belongs here it's me!

JENNY. For gossips to come look? You have to leave. I have to think only of my grandson.

FRANCINE. What about my baby?

JENNY. If you stay – the disgrace – my Leo will never return.

*(***FRANCINE** *stands and confronts her face to face.)*

FRANCINE. But what about my baby?

JENNY. It's too much now for a young boy.

FRANCINE. I've made many concessions to you –

JENNY. Me? You no do it for me. For me everything is dead. Gone!

FRANCINE. I'm not going to leave.

JENNY. You want to sit?

FRANCINE. Yes!

*(***JENNY** *grabs a folding chair and slams it down where the casket should sit.)*

JENNY. Sit! We get another big chair. When the television comes, we all laugh. You, me –

(ref: **CONNIE** *and* **ROSA***)*

quella due stronze – the pope, everybody! *(Tr: Those two turds)*

FRANCINE. I don't want anyone to laugh.

JENNY. Then what do you want? If you love my Joey, you leave. You love him, you won't hurt his son.

*(***JENNY*** returns to her seat next to* **CONNIE** *and stares straight ahead.* **FRANCINE** *returns to her seat in front row/second set and contemplates her next move. Her eyes dart to the plastic gladioli, to the folding chair* **JENNY** *planted, to* **CONNIE** *who is staring down at the papers clutched in her hands.)*

*(***FRANCINE*** slowly rises, crosses to the remembrance card table and takes one. She then crosses back to her chair and fumbles with her purse as she places the remembrance card inside it. After a moment's hesitation, she picks up her sweater and presses it to her chest. As she looks down at* **JENNY***,* **ROSA***, and* **CONNIE***…)*

FRANCINE. Fine!

*(***FRANCINE*** heads for the main exit. As she opens one of the doors, the room fills with the muffled voices coming from the packed lobby.* **CONNIE** *bolts up!)*

ROSA. *(grabbing* **CONNIE***'s arm)* Connie!

*(***CONNIE*** releases herself from her mother's grip and rushes over to* **FRANCINE** *with the divorce papers.)*

CONNIE. Here, this is yours.

(Puzzled **FRANCINE** *slowly opens the envelope, and as she reads the funny message on the greeting card, she laughs unintentionally. As she carefully opens it the divorce papers fall to the floor.* **CONNIE** *drops down and quickly retrieves them and places them back into* **FRANCINE***'s hands. While* **FRANCINE** *reads the divorce papers her eyes flick back and forth to* **CONNIE***'s. When she's*

*read enough, she clutches them in her fist and runs from the room. **CONNIE** gently closes the door and presses her head against it.)*

ROSA. Connie, sit down!

*(A robotic **CONNIE** crosses back to big chair and sits very still.)*

(standing)

I'll go call Uncle Johnny.

*(Before leaving **ROSA** crosses behind **CONNIE** and puts the veil back over her face.)*

*(to **JENNY**)*

You did the right thing.

JENNY. *(with disdain)* Rosa, make your call!

*(As **ROSA** heads towards the main lobby **CONNIE** puts her hands under the veil and covers her face, then lowers her head down into her lap. As **ROSA** opens a door and is greeted by the loud clamor out in the lobby – **BERNARD** appears in the doorway carrying **FRANCINE**'s "Bleeding Heart" – a large heart-shaped floral arrangement on a tall stand covered in red American Beauty roses and with a banner reading "With all my love." As he enters he almost knocks a stunned **ROSA** down, but she bounces back and grabs hold of the flower arrangement and reads the card. As she reads an impatient **BERNARD** yanks them away and crosses to the front of the room.)*

*(As a shrewd **ROSA** exits she makes a subtle hand gesture that says she'll deal with **BERNARD** and the flowers later. **SAMMY** enters through the open main door, closes it behind him and the room grows quiet. He then crosses to the smoking alcove. **BERNARD** plops the "Bleeding Heart" down next to the plastic gladioli, then quickly picks up the plastic arrangement and crosses to the smoking alcove. **JENNY** stares up at the "Bleeding Heart" and cries softly.)*

SAMMY. *(whispered)* Bernard, I'll be right down.

(**BERNARD** *exits with the plastic gladioli down the private hall.* **SAMMY** *adjusts his suit and tie, stands erect, walks very slowly down to the casket area and takes the folding chair* **JENNY** *placed and puts it back in its rightful place. He then crosses to* **JENNY**.)

SAMMY. *(cont.) Signora Barbalottio, scusi. Siamo pronto. (Tr: Mrs. Barbalottio, excuse me. We're ready.)*

(**JENNY** *immediately brushes away her tears.*)

Può aspettare dentro la stanza privata? (Tr: Would you care to wait in the private hall?)

(**SAMMY** *helps a stoic* **JENNY** *from her chair, and slowly crosses with her to a chair in the smoking alcove.*)

Era una buona persona, e un buon amico. Dio lo benedica. Dio lo benedica.(Tr: He was a good person and a good friend. God bless him, God bless him.)

(*Once* **JENNY** *is safely seated,* **SAMMY** *crosses to* **CONNIE**.)

Mrs. Barbalottio!

(**CONNIE** *sits up.*)

If there's anything you want, just ask. You don't like something, tell me. That's what I'm here for. The air-conditioning too high?

(**SAMMY** *helps* **CONNIE** *out of her seat, and in true undertaker fashion, takes her under the arm and tries to direct her towards the smoking alcove. As they cross the casket area,* **CONNIE** *pauses and stares at "The Bleeding Heart.")*

Don't be nervous.

(*And with that* **CONNIE** *gently sobs.*)

You'll be all right.

(*As* **SAMMY** *pats* **CONNIE** *affectionately on the back she sobs even more.*)

It's good to let it out of your system.

(As the masterful **SAMMY** *moves a weak-kneed* **CONNIE** *to the smoking alcove…)*

SAMMY. *(cont.)* I understand. I understand.

*(***SAMMY*** *sits the sobbing* **CONNIE** *in a chair next to the unsympathetic* **JENNY**. *Now content that all is proper,* **SAMMY** *exits down the private hall leaving the room filled with the sound of the tragic* **CONNIE**'s *sobs and the eerie sound of the approaching service elevator. The lights fade, leaving a key light to enhance the "Bleeding Heart" floral arrangement.)*

*(**IT IS SUGGESTED THAT**: Billy Joel's instrumental version of his "New York State of Mind" be played as the curtain falls and during the curtain calls.)*

(curtain)

PROPERTIES LIST

Preset Offstage:

In the service elevator: A bronze casket on its rolling beir. An American flag - freshly pressed - folded across the casket's center. *(For* **BERNARD** *and* **SAMMY**.*)*

The second trip in the service elevator: A spray of white plastic gladioli on a tall pedestal, a wooden kneeler and an easy chair. *(For* **BERNARD**.*)*

The third trip in the service elevator. An upholstered kneeler. *(For* **BERNARD**.*)*

Rememberance cards. The size of a playing card, one side has a picture of a religious figure or religious scene, the other side a short prayer, the name of the deceased, his or her birth and death dates. *(For* **BERNARD**.*)*

A guest register and pen. *(For* **BERNARD**.*)*

A damp cloth. *(For* **MARYANNE**.*)*

A paper cup filled with whiskey. *(For* **SAMMY**.*)*

The "Bleeding Heart" floral arrangement. A heart-shaped floral piece on tall pedestal. Roses outlined with baby's breath, the whole framed with palm leaves. Narrow satin ribbons cascading down the front. Flowers and ribbons should be red. *(For* **BERNANRD**.*)*

The Set:

10 wooden folding chairs stacked in the main room.

A dust rag on top of one of the chairs.

Two occasional chairs already in place in the smoking alcove.

Ash trays in place in the smoking alcove.

A stand to hold the guest register. In place in the main room.

A remembrance card table (a small round wooden table) with the funeral director's cards and calendars on top of it. It is downstage to the smoking alcove.

A large wooden cross should hang on the draperies at stage right.

COSTUME LIST

FRANCINE:
> A polka-dot maternity dress, 6th month pregnancy pouch, slip, stockings, shoes, purse, and a large dark blue men's sweater with a NYPD patch.

CONNIE:
> Black dress *(a designer knock-off)* slip, grey-black hose, black evening shoes, wedding band, traditional mourning veil, a wristwatch, and a black purse *(borrowed from her mother.)*

MARYANNE:
> Salon smock, uniform pants, panty hose, shoes, wig, purse, headscarf, wedding band, and earrings.

PHYLLIS:
> Salon smock, uniform pants, panty hose, shoes, wig, purse, tote bag, and headscarf.

ROSA:
> A frumpy black dress, corset, slip, black stockings, black wedgies, a large black purse, and a wedding band.

JENNY:
> A conservative black dress, slip, black stockings, black lace-up shoes, black purse, black handkercheif, and a wedding band.

SAMMY:
> A dark conservative three piece suit, shoes, shirt, tie, socks, pocket handkercheif, and a wristwatch.

BERNARD:
> A dark suit, shoes, shirt, cufflnks, tie, socks, and a ring.

PERSONAL PROPS

For **FRANCINE:** Tissues. One or two bobby pins in her hair.

For **CONNIE:** Cigarettes and matches.

For **MARYANNE:** A box of tissues and a comb.

For **PHYLLIS:** A hairbrush, a pack of Camel cigarettes, matches, a newspaper on the line of the *Star* or *The Enquirer*, a bottle of pills, a comb, and a Rosary.

For **ROSA:** A hairbrush, tissues, "Lifesavers", coin purse and coins.

For **JENNY:** Divorce papers folded in a greeting card with its envelope addressed to Francine.

For **SAMMY:** Cigarettes and a lighter.

For **BERNARD:** None.

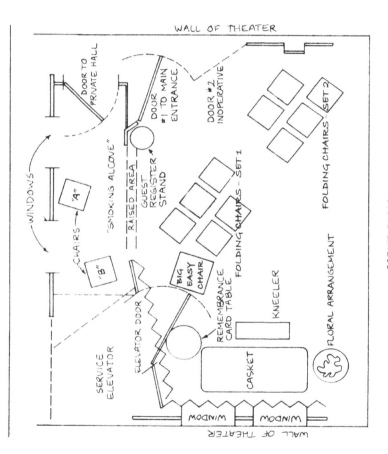

SCENE DESIGN
"AMIDST THE GLADIOLAS"

OTHER TITLES AVAILABLE FROM SAMUEL FRENCH

THE ALTOS

David Landau
Music & Lyrics by Nikki Stern

4m, 3f / Full Length / Musical Comedy / Interior

Like 'The Sopranos', only lower!

An Interactive Musical Comedy Mystery Spoof of the famous HBO series. Meet the family that inspired it all, the Altos. It's Tony's funeral (Or is it?) and his wife Toffee has invited you to the wake. Chris wants you should check your weapons at the door (and if you don't have any, he's got extras!) Uncle Senior has a rigged dice game going and Tony's Ma is - well just nuts. Tony's shrink Dr. Malaise is giving free analysis and the Father isn't sure what he is doing! But one thing is for sure, almost no one seems sad that Tony is gone and they certainly done seem happy once he's discovered alive. Be prepared to dodge bullets, laugh at the songs and see if you can't figure out who put a contract out on Tony!

OTHER TITLES AVAILABLE FROM SAMUEL FRENCH

WHERE THERE'S A WILL, THERE'S A RELATIVE

Roger Karshner

Comedy / 3m, 3f / Interior

Sam Price, a wealthy entrepreneur, has just recently passed away and, at his request, has been laid out in his townhouse. With the corpse in the bedroom, his immediate family—sister, brother, nephew and niece—have gathered to discuss their inheritance, a meeting that descends into acrimony over the division of property. Much to their chagrin, they learn that Sam has left his entire estate to the church, a discovery that results in them reluctantly seeking the advice of a person they deem to be of unsavory moral character. His advice seemingly solves their dilemma until they realize that the solution involves compromise. Many reversals drive a story that comically reveals avarice, mistrust and chicanery.

Lightning Source UK Ltd.
Milton Keynes UK
UKOW06f0254030615

252796UK00001B/14/P